ACCLAIM FOR
Driving Men Mad

"Audacious. . . . There's hardly a word in [these stories] that doesn't weigh heavily, or doesn't have a bristling edge to it."
                                                    – *Toronto Star*

"Levine's vivid language and unflinching exploration of people living on the edge of society will stay with you long after each story is read. . . . Her explorations of humanity and the adventurous spirit of her work will keep the reader hooked, hesitating to turn the page but unable to resist the pull of her prose."
                                – *St. John's Evening Telegram*

"Levine's writing is adventurous and brave. . . . Tautly constructed and rigorously controlled. . . ."
                                                    – *Quill & Quire*

"Levine's writing compresses the distance between art and audience, drawing a reader experientially through her fiction. She is a visceral imagist. Her fiction renders event indistinguishable from emotion, affecting the gut as fully as the mind. . . ."
                                            – *Ottawa Citizen*

"No reader can make his or her way through these stories and retain any kind of complacency."
                                                    – *Calgary Herald*

BOOKS BY ELISE LEVINE

Driving Men Mad (1995)
Requests and Dedications (2003)

ELISE LEVINE

DRIVING

MEN

MAD

EMBLEM EDITIONS
Published by McClelland & Stewart Ltd.

Copyright © 1995 by Elise Levine

First published in trade paperback by The Porcupine's Quill Inc., 1995
First Emblem Editions publication 2003

National Library of Canada Cataloguing in Publication

Levine, Elise, 1959–
Driving men mad / Elise Levine.

ISBN 0-7710-5279-0

I. Title.

PS8573.E9647D73 2004   C813'.54   C2003-901798-2
PR9199.3.L4675D75 2004

We acknowledge the financial support of the Government of Canada through
the Book Publishing Industry Development Program and that of the
Government of Ontario through the Ontario Media Development
Corporation's Ontario Book Initiative. We further acknowledge the
support of the Canada Council for the Arts and the
Ontario Arts Council for our publishing program.

The lyrics on pages 90-91 are taken from FLIPPER, by Henry Vars and
By Dunham © 1963 Metro-Goldwyn-Mayer Inc. and Ivan Tors Films Inc.
© Renewed EMI Feist Catalog Inc. All Rights Reserved. Used by
Permission. WARNER BROS. PUBLICATIONS U.S. INC., Miami, FL. 33014

SERIES EDITOR: ELLEN SELIGMAN

Cover design: Terri Nimmo
Cover image © Lisa Spindler / Graphistock
Series logo design: Brian Bean

Typeset in Bembo by M&S, Toronto
Printed and bound in Canada

This book is printed on acid-free paper that is 100% recycled,
ancient forest friendly (40% post-consumer recycled).

EMBLEM EDITIONS
McClelland & Stewart Ltd.
The Canadian Publishers
481 University Avenue
Toronto, Ontario
M5G 2E9
www.mcclelland.com/emblem

1   2   3   4   5   07   06   05   04   03

For Helen Humphreys

Contents

Angel

It was midnight, Angel, and I'll never forget. We did it in doorways up and down Church Street, my back against rotting wood or my hamstrings hurting, crouched down on grey concrete, the club where I'd cruised you receding as we twisted down alleyways and across half-empty parking lots. You wooed me that night and I could hear my breath whistling in and out of me and when you pulled my shirt up and over my head and tossed it – just like that, in the middle of the street – it was like a ghost floated up inside me and fluttered out of my mouth, my white shirt sailing up over Parliament Street, and the next morning I saw it lying on the streetcar tracks at Queen and Sherbourne.

We were already light-years away from everything I thought I knew (I was fresh off the bus from Owen Sound) and we never stopped once, skidding through the rain-slick streets of Rosedale at three in the morning or standing under the fluorescent hum of all-night pizza joints, hungry (we were so hungry). Or the night you turned a trick and next morning we took the Bathurst Street bus to Starkman's Surgical Supplies. You gave me the guided tour, row upon immaculate row of enema equipment, the smell of the rubber gloves you pressed to my face, and the shiny steel clamp you bought for seventy dollars. That night you pierced my right nipple – for love, you said, as I handed you the surgical steel ring – and that photographer documented it, then threw us out when we ripped through her cupboard for food.

I had walked into the city, Angel.

I never looked back.

Farmers were torching peaches in the Golden Horseshoe that summer. Though substandard – too small – they smelled overripe and bursting with a faint odour of gasoline underneath and we lived on them for a month because they cost next to nothing. I sold some blow in the bars and bought a beat-up Chevy Nova for five hundred dollars, and we'd drive it out of the city to where it was dry and dusty, the late-August fields burning with goldenrod. We'd stop on dirt roads and my eyelids would sweat as I squinted against the two o'clock sun, and when you kissed me I remembered how it felt when you pushed the needle through the cork and carefully threaded the ring through me and I didn't flinch, only squeezed my eyes half-shut against the pain and flushed cold-hot.

That's when you were there for me most, saying, Your aureole, aurora, bright aura burning pink-gold; and the single bead of blood below my nipple made me think of my heart beating fast and clear underneath.

We'd drive real slow through Stouffville, then stop at Musselman's Lake to swim. And when you laid me on my stomach in the grass I was afraid of getting caught, I knew the bikers at Musselman's could be pretty rough trade and I knew exactly what they might do but we did it anyway, we always did it anyway.

And that was a little like what happened with Nancy Smith and me when we were sixteen and we did it anyway and paid the price, Lezzie Cunt scratched on my locker at school or the night I drove my dad's car to the Esso off Main Street and Ken Hale and his older brother and their friends were there, standing around their pick-ups and Camaros and I felt a little nervous but I got out of the car and walked over to the pump and took down the hose and slowly unscrewed the gas cap and very carefully filled the tank but out of the corner of my eye I could see one of the guys rubbing his dick and when he saw me notice him he said, Look at her look, she knows I've got what she needs. I carefully put the hose back but by then they were all walking over so I got in the car and slammed the door shut, I never stopped to pay the bill, just made a fast left out of there and it wasn't till I was halfway home that I smelled the gas and realized I'd dropped the gas cap at the station and I was spilling tracks all the way down Main that night.

But you and me always did it anyway, Angel, and in the evening we'd drive back along the 400 doing a cool 140, slipping in and out of one long stream of tail lights past Barrie, the long ride home like the strong fluid lines of a game of pool I'd seen you play one Saturday night in July at the old Cameo Club off Eastern Avenue. You'd just started taking me around, and the bouncer at the door that night had wanted to see my I.D. but you said, It's okay, Val, and she hissed, Baby dyke, at me under her breath and let me pass. You racked up those balls like a pro and beat those old dykes in their black leather vests who lovingly took their hand-crafted, mother-of-pearl-inlaid cues from monogrammed cases and everyone stood around, and I counted each sudden click as you knocked the balls down, always where you said you wanted them and it was like each click that night brought me closer to something, each click a notch cut closer through the tension thick as the blue smoky bar or the heavenly sweet smell of amyl in the bathroom, and looking up I could see the smooth moves shaking it out there on the dance floor but all I could hear was you, calling, Six ball in the corner pocket, and click, Nine ball in the side pocket, and all night long I felt I was moving, Angel, really moving.

It was like you were some kind of angel from outer space, and I was strung out on some serious religious songs like your heart had all this voodoo over me. But you became featherlight; and in what became that wet summer city at night – the bars emptying – you had left hours earlier with someone else, and the street lights seemed leprous, yellow like old age and neglect, like bright nimbuses of neglect.

Remember when we stole that van? Coked up and joyriding the 401 at four in the morning, we thought we'd get as far as Montreal then ditch the sucker. You were driving so fast, bouncing us between semis, each one carrying a single cargo of cowboy hurtling through the tail end of a four-day run and I was riding fast and scared, a little slick between my legs and you were talking non-stop, saying we'd do this and then that, adventures, always big adventures and when you rolled the van a little ways out past Kingston I just held on tight and never screamed once.

Now I'm here in this hospital, Angel, because (forgive me) I tried to let you go. Three days ago they pumped my stomach, its shiny stinking freight of two hundred assorted Christmas Trees and Percodans. Now they send round the therapists and social workers, the students from Abnormal Psych 101 and there are things they want to hear but I know it's what they think they already know so I squeeze my eyes tight in concentration and I tell them nothing. *Queer girl*.

And this nothing but this light in my head.

So touch me. Touch me before I die of old age. I'm out on the street corner and the light haloes me and I'm waiting for you with my young lean body, its barely learned distrust of strangers.

So this is how I think of you, Angel.

The van's on fire and we're sitting in the ditch watching and I can feel the hot breath of escape on my face. You stand up and sway slightly from the effort then you walk out onto the shoulder and keep on going. And although I never see you again I'm still waiting by the side of the 401, waiting through the hot sting of freezing rain or the claustral breath of August and as each car screams past I lift my head to look for you, but it's never you, Angel. Never you.

But sometimes I think maybe you're here with me now, only we're out there, joyriding the lights glowing blue-black on wet summer streets or else we're driving easy with the windows down all the way and we're counting car headlights strung like pearls across the highway, and I keep thinking there's a city here somewhere but sometimes I find it a struggle to believe – but I do believe, Angel, I swear I do – and it's like I can almost see lights rocking across a harbour while the round earth's rocking and calling to us, and it's funny but I can remember being in the back seat of a car when

I was really little and being rocked to sleep by the motion, and right now I can feel the top of my skull nasty and bubbling with amphetamines. And yours too, sure. Yours too.

In Marble

As things unfold I am one of the first. Up from the summer city loaded like dice all July long, I came out of the heat to the hush and blur of wing tip against wave. The cliff wall glowed pink in moonlight, a thick granite wedged against sky, rock scaling cliffs of wind to rise out of Lake Mazinaw with its fabled monsters I found to be only sturgeon, and the small female crayfish white-grey and blistered with babies, and the ling cod big in summer as Cadillacs.

Steve Miles'd been with me earlier, sidemount diving inside Marble Cave, an underwater river cave ten minutes down the road from Mazinaw. Two ninety-five-cubic-foot steel tanks, one on each side instead of on the back, twenty-one-pound battery canister for the primary hand-held Neutralite tacked below the ass, and everything (regulators, hoses, pressure gauges, backup lights, *everything*) tight up to the body to keep the profile down: I'd learned to sidemount only that winter, from the sidemount kings of Florida. Those old boys could skinny through the nastiest restrictions.

Here I was one of the first. Fucking Canadians. Most never do a thing, either it costs too much or the government won't let them.

I'd done surveying in Marble, and installed permanent line there. (One of the rules of cave diving that's cast in stone: Always run a continuous guideline to the surface. In the mazed world of a cave, that line's your ball of string enabling your safe return; it's your highway to the new world, and back to the old.)

I was taking Steve in for his first experience at crunch diving. We'd hooked up at Underwater Canada, the dive industry trade show, that spring. He wanted, he'd said, to expand his horizons, get some experience. Marble's a good place to learn since it only goes in about four hundred feet, and it's shallow, mostly ten feet deep. And since the deeper you go underwater the more air you breathe, if you got stuck in Marble you'd have all day to get yourself out.

Anyone bought it here they'd deserve it.

Steve and I were going back the next day. I assumed we'd share a motel room, maybe my tent, that night.

At five o'clock, almost finished loading up the trucks, he clears his throat.

Beyond the stand of aspen and a sprinkling of birch, a partridge flurried her three chicks away from us, along the path toward the water's edge. I still had to make one more trip back down there to get the last of my gear: a helmet with three small backup Sabrelights attached, and my fins. I was tired.

Steve cleared his throat again.

Gonna stay with a girlfriend in Belleville, he goes. Catch you tomorrow. Breakfast around ten?

I nod, *yes*. Then I go (and my voice goes up my nose, and I'm surprised), I go, Belleville's a long haul.

Even though it isn't really.

During the dive I'd held up my backup regulator, hit the purge button, and blown an air pocket into the ceiling of the small room twenty feet from the end of the line. I ascended, flashing my light to get Steve's attention. I waved my arm, *up*.

What do you think?

His eyes almost as big as his mask.

I said it again: What do you think?

In the air his breath shook and rattled his regulator. Wouldn't take it out of his mouth.

Half in, half out of water, wet marble everywhere around us. I was looking at him squeezed into this smallest moment, with only the two of us knowing it.

Can't get any closer than this.

•

By six that night I was eating liver and onions by myself at Heather's, a restaurant on Highway 41, overlooking Lake Mazinaw, on the outskirts of Bon Echo Provincial Park. At eleven, starting to wake up a bit – and (story of my life) bored and more bored – I left my tent I'd pitched at a campsite near the water. I went to the truck, set up a single tank, walked down the path by flashlight. Swam on the surface over to the cliff wall, dropped to a hundred and ten feet. When I saw what there was to see I surfaced, went back, and got my doubles. Did a real dive.

Most of my life I was mostly solo. For example: at three in the morning, cold in my sleeping bag, hands pressed tight between my thighs. Imagining the stars groaning in the sky outside my tent, wondering how it came to be that the only times I seemed to get fucked it was by myself, on a dive. All the mistakes I ever made.

Should've died a million times over.

In the morning Steve was nowhere. Didn't show at Heather's for breakfast.

I drove over to Marble. The water cool, uncold; the day before I'd taken a reading of 69° F. Sunfish blurred the cave mouth. The river was down, running slow. In spite of everything, I was feeling pretty good.

The partridge we'd seen the day before fussed in the trees. Mosquitoes jabbed my cheeks until I pulled on my hood.

I'd figured Steve would be a no-show.

I certainly went too far. Like Jurgen, best of the best, *they broke the mould*: only last year, when his body surfaced on its own without him in a cave in Mexico, broken apart coming up from the thousand-foot scuba record he was going for – his nervous system shut down at depth, his entire body probably shaking, vision impaired by the explosions of black concentric rings he described experiencing on his 863-foot dive at Bushmansgat, South Africa – his support team (friends and family among them) was turning away for lack of a body bag in which to place his remains and finish the recovery. Trying to get out of there fast, before the media showed up. Not crying. Could have been anyone.

Reduced to this.

Dave Kellar and I once went back about seven thousand feet in Dos Ojos, a mostly freshwater *cenote*, a spring cave formed by an underground river, in the Yucatan. (In terms of the overall system, seven grand's nothing: Dave and the others have pushed about ninety thousand feet of passage over the years, and it's still *going*.)

Another rule that's cast in stone is the rule of thirds: Breathe only a third of your air in, reserving a third to exit and a third to share in case of emergency. Never go past your thirds, unless you want to end up as one of the swimming dead.

In fact I was using a dead man's gear. The National Speleological Society, Cave Diving Section had flown me from Tampa to drive the guy's truck home, also his dog, but that's another story, as is exactly how he came to pass from this world convulsing 302 feet deep in a cave near Merida.

Dave and I'd gone in on the main line in Dos Ojos using scooters – motorized DPVs, dive propulsion vehicles that allow you to, in this case, at least quadruple the distance you could cover just swimming. Mark Moore'd gone in ahead of us to survey a new passage off the main line. Having breathed a third of each of our double-stage bottles (eighty-cubic-foot tanks worn on each side of the body), Dave and I stopped to drop them with our scooters, which had enough battery power left to allow us to exit. From there we continued, breathing from our backmounted double 104s, turning off the main line onto a tee.

I've heard people call the water in freshwater caves *sweetwater*. Wasn't sweet on this dive: up and down from zero to thirty, occasionally fifty feet – my sinuses killing me with all the pressure changes – and with this dead guy's gear nothing felt quite right.

When I reached my turn-pressure I signalled Dave and called the dive. But when we came back to what should have been the main line, with a single plastic line arrow we'd placed there, marking the direction out – like most Mexican caves Dos Ojos is heavily decorated with formations contributing to the complexity of its numerous, mazy passages – we instead found a junction with several almost indistinguishable lines, wrapped together around a stalagmite. Couldn't see where one ended and another began. And instead of a single line arrow, there was a second arrow, pointing in another direction. Clipped to all three lines was a slate that read: Shortest Way to Air Good Luck Getting Out.

We were too far in to swim out. We had to have those scooters and stages to complete our exit, otherwise we'd run out of air. Worse, this place was so shallow you could be swimming dead, *knowing* you'd never make it, for hours.

Dave moved within inches of the line junction, looked close. He rose several feet, moved away, came back in. Finally he pointed, *This way*.

Every few hundred feet or so I flashed my light and when he turned to look at me, I yelled into my regulator. *You sure?*

At first he wouldn't look me in the eye, just glanced down at the line then away, then back again at the line.

Each time we stopped like this he'd finally look at me again, slowly point and nod. This way.

We went up. We went down. We came to our first stage bottles.

In the van heading back to Tulúm, Mark explained his note. He'd run a line into a passage that gave out only two hundred feet in, at a sink open to air from above, but the walls of which were too steep to climb out. Had Dave and I chosen that line, doubling back that distance wouldn't have killed us.

Drops of rain big as frogs squashed against the van's windshield. I leaned forward from the back seat.

Dave, I said. How'd you know which line to choose?

He didn't turn around, and in the smashing rain I wasn't sure if he answered or not.

Mexico was years later. Unlike most Mexican caves, Marble is simple. Main line. Single tee. Shallow. Only goes back about four hundred feet.

I slugged my tanks along the path. The water cool, uncold. Fat bullheads and rock bass, and small brightly coloured pumpkinseeds, slurred from the mouth of the cave. The river was down, running slow.

Not more than a hundred feet inside, just past the big room (big only in relation to everything else in Marble),

I somehow got off the main line and onto the tee, without realizing. In fact I'd forgotten altogether about the other line, even though I'd laid it myself three months earlier, through a passage so tight and nasty I had to remove both tanks and push one in front of me to get through, gripping the regulator so tight in my teeth for fear of dropping the tank I thought I might break the silicone nipples off.

Tight. So tight in places my chest had barely room enough to let me breathe. I was confused: nothing looked familiar. Amazing how much a person can forget. I went as far as I could without having to take my tanks off. Seemed like a long time. When I finally stopped I was wedged in so good it took at least five minutes just to turn around, scratching and clawing and grinding against rock (hoping I wouldn't cut a hose or knock a tank valve or tear off a pressure gauge and lose my air), and another ten to come back the thirty feet to the main line. Not swimming: crawling. Blind in the silt.

In Dos Ojos, in Areolito de Paraiso, in Carwash, Temple of Doom – in the sweetwater *cenotes* of Mexico: a-thousand-foot-plus visibility. Seeing forever. Sweet water. Not like in Marble, all the dirty shit washing over you, everything you've stirred up.

Coming out in zero visibility: on the line, touch contact with an interlocking O made by the thumb and middle finger, feeling your way out blind through cuspids of rock, pulling the line out of line traps. Barely squeaking through the largest part of each restriction.

Question is: Would two heads have been better than one? Didn't even realize my mistake until I got back to the main line and thought, Which way?

There are times when everything comes down to this: maximum stupid, all the way out. Like the river that day: down and slow.

The river was down, running slow.

Sometimes the river was up. Ottawa, even in August. Spring caves like Madison and Jackson, blowing blue.

Before the flooding starts and the river backs up.

As things unfold over the years I strung together dive after dive. I thought I could go farther each time because experience, I learned, is everything, one thing adding up to another in the same way I could count on some Jeanie or some Ted and in the end never really know what they were made of. Story of my life: sometimes I got lucky, got hurt, and lived. End of story. I lost those near to me through the usual etceteras, separation, divorce. I lived. I lost Johnny Sheppard in downstream Clearcut one night, swimming its hundred-foot-high white walls and scalloped false floors, trying to make the traverse to Venture Sink. We'd done the system together so many times we were doing visuals, not stopping to run gap reels between the jumps.

Two days later the recovery team found him at twenty-five feet, pinned to the ceiling, his 104s and stage bottle empty. Came down to this: he must have panicked when he realized he'd missed a jump, and begun to hoover back his air like there was no tomorrow. I'd looked for him as long as I could that night, before time ran out.

Shoulda run a line.

Since for Jeanie or for Johnny-any-Johnny – all the Johnnies – we go too far. We can only go so far.

I lived. I lived.

Mostly solo.

And the others, remember them? the hardcores, the wannabes, the scooter animals on deep-modified DPVs imploding at the talus mound during a two a.m. sneak-dive in Sally Ward at Wakulla Springs (entering the river we'd used only our penlights to check for alligators, not wanting to alert the warden to our presence and end up in the crowbar motel). Shooting semi-feral cats, pow-pow, each one bred for target practice except the one Gary Brooks just moved down from Maryland shot by mistake, that one was Pete Martin's favourite tabby bitch he used to lure all the toms and Gary trying so hard to fit in.

We knew how to have fun. Kick ass inside miles of phreatic tunnel twisting through solid rock like a nerve, like a filament of light where we systematically pushed back the darkness of karst terrain – and always, passage *still* going, forged a billion years ago out of the blood of heated rock heaving and puking itself into formation. Wearing all this cyborgian gear and coming soon now these rebreathers (*deeper, harder*) and one day there'll be gill implants. *If only.* Because around two hundred and thirty feet breathing air your breath sounds like wind chimes, at two-fifty the blood in your body an audible coursing, the high-pitched whine of an engine, lulling you so deep your bubbles the only thing singing you awake so you learn gas switches, breathing trimix, heliox to keep the Charybdis and Scylla of nitrogen narcosis and oxygen toxicity at bay. Beneath hundreds of pounds and twenty thousand dollars' worth of gear (redundancy, redundancy, redundancy): you. You in your sudden joy knowing you're doing it: making the dive. Hinting of other futures.

Mostly solo.

Being first.

Wanting everything. Risking all.

Remembering all those for whom time ran out including the father and son whose ashes cave divers scattered just beyond the Heinkel restriction in Devil's Eye at Ginnie Springs, a true story. All as things unfold. All the things you learn and the most you learn is from your mistakes, if you survive them. The tee'd line in Marble in hard complacent Ontario where my mother and father forged me out of their Maritime-exiled hope (jobs, education, opportunity knocking, knocking – though every chance I got I turned inward, further in).

The terrible price of all things.

Broke the mould: a new breed, a vanishing breed (magazines and newspapers say anything). Those that do and those that don't, and some who only shoot their mouths off. Exploration: those that have the right to and no one to tell them otherwise. Those that have the right.

Wanting everything.

Another rule: Never exceed your limits.

Whatever that last one means.

As things unfold I was as I say up from the summer city loaded like dice all July long. In the morning as at night the wall at Mazinaw glowed pink, a thick granite wedged against sky. I drove over to Marble. The water cool, uncold. Sunfish slurring from the mouth of the cave. The river was down, running slow. I carried my tanks along the path. No longer any sign of the partridge or her brood among the still trees. And Steve, I thought. And then I thought, So fuck him.

Marble's simple. But I was alone and feeling cocky and that'll do it every time, only this was the first time I knew it for sure.

Face, ass, breasts, every part of me equalling this: stuck in rock. Tangling and untangling in the line. Feeling my way out blind as Tiresias. Knowing for the first time how easily I could slip into my skin. Become, briefly, a swimming dead thing.

Knowing I could never be more alive than this.

And I am one of those.

As the story goes the last time I fucked up in a cave it was big time. Four thousand feet back in Devil's Eye – I'd been laying line in Main Land – must have missed the second tee out. Took a while to realize I'd gone too far. I was breathing thirds, then halves. I stopped calculating. I'd found, I believed, the quickest way out. I believed I was finally in for it.

Sweetwater, ride of my life.

Retiring·

When Bobbie lies in bed at night, she can feel her skin crawl. After thirty-one years of living in Brampton, she no longer notices new-house sounds, the settlings and creakings once as heart-stopping as groans. Instead, she lies awake and stares at the spot where three years ago Larry patched the ceiling with plaster of Paris but never painted, now frilling and flaking around the edges, and she thinks her skin looks just like that. Bobbie imagines she might hear it one night, her skin quietly slithering from her body, unwrapping from her like something alive and breathing and hugging her with decreasing tautness the past fifty-eight years, and now slipping from her while the electric clock thrums downstairs in the kitchen, time slipping from her body in gauzy strips.

So she's a little nervous, and when in his sleep Larry rolls over onto his back Bobbie thinks one of these nights that ceiling will fall down and hope to hell it lands on

Larry's head, because that'll teach him not to leave things too long.

The specialists say it's a rare and incurable form of psoriasis – caused by years of exposure to cosmetics and aggravated, now, by stress – and they can't really help her, which is what they told her when she took a morning off from Eaton's and Larry closed the shoe store and drove her to Toronto General for her appointment. They were both a little jumpy, and Larry said, You don't have to bite my head off, Bobbie, after he drove around the block at College and University *three* times looking for a parking meter and when he finally found one on College and slowed down to park, a streetcar driver clanged at him and Larry, who just hated driving downtown, had moved on.

But then he had looked so ill at ease in the clinic waiting room that Bobbie almost had to laugh. That was her Larry, she thought.

When it was Bobbie's turn to see Dr. Lee he took her thick achy hands in his and Bobbie looked down and away. He didn't say much, an Oriental and it's true, they're so quiet you never know what they're thinking. Still, he touched her hands lightly, lightly running his fingertips across her nails, then putting his face an inch from her index finger and examining every nook and cranny in the cracks between each tender digit.

Maybe he's just a little shy, Bobbie thinks, and when Dr. Lee turns her hands palm up she cautiously looks at his face; and when he suddenly looks her in the eye she's caught off guard and gives a little jump.

There's nothing we can do for you, he had said.

And, as Bobbie told each lousy doctor in turn, it hurts, too. So Bobbie's nervous, very nervous. She tosses and turns in bed until four, knowing that when she gets up for work in the morning the sheets will be covered with thin white flakes, and while Larry showers she'll bundle up the bedclothes and take them downstairs to the basement, and put them in the washing machine. Then she'll go upstairs to the kitchen and put the coffee on.

Annette walks by Men's Cosmetics at ten-fifteen and winks at Bobbie. Bobbie tilts her head exactly one-quarter of an inch over the rows of green and black bottles of cologne in reply and without missing a beat reaches down to the glass case in front of her and pulls out a three-ounce box of talc for Mr. Pauley, whose tender after-shaving face Bobbie has helped soothe going on twelve years now. She knows she calms him, makes it easy for a man to walk over to Cosmetics and say hello, to place his gloves on the glass counter, so natural to discuss his intimate grooming needs with this woman, her voice slightly deep and mannish but, still, a blonde looker who's never brassy: this class act.

Sometimes, though, Bobbie's bleached moustache beads with sweat under the hot store lights, especially when Mr. Hoban follows Mr. Elliott (they both love to talk), and a young man Bobbie's never seen before wants service right away (even though Mary's not back from her break yet), and they *all* want cologne, nail brushes, whatever's on special promotion this week and free.

Annette will come to the counter again, at twelve, and the two women will ride the escalator up to Arcadian Court on Seven.

The girls are over there, by the window, two tables to the left of the chandelier. The room's filled to the rafters with elderly ladies, their blue hair topped by royal blue or burgundy velvet turbans garnished with feathers or rhinestones. They're like brightly coloured balloons bobbing around the room, and any moment now Mr. Clown will appear and someone will reach up and honk his nose and he'll feign first surprise and then tears, poor Mr. Clown, so funny and sad he'd make people laugh till they cried. Bobbie feels giddy, a little silly so she'll have to watch herself, she thinks, these women so elegant with their lavender or white cotton gloves (of course, gloves) lunching here because it reminds them of something, of the ballet and beef Wellington and sherry trifle for dessert – the grandeur of this place where matrons in support hose serve and assist – and the ladies remind Bobbie of her grandmother, they seem so old.

Jean says, Hey, old doll, and Bobbie clacks her tray next to Sheila's and sits down.

Bobbie prods her chicken pot pie and Annette shakes her head and says, Putting another old one out to pasture.

Sheila says, So how's it feel, Bobbie? – your last three days!

Bobbie takes a deep breath, looks to her left out the window at Old City Hall, turns her head back and folds her hands as if saying grace for the green Jell-O with passionfruit lying before her. Then she rolls her eyes upward – thank you, lord, thank you – and the girls laugh.

On the escalator down to Three Below, Annette says, Bobbie, you don't look too bad today. You doing a little better?

Bobbie appreciates Annette's caution, all light concern even though it's spreading. And Bobbie ticks off the list: first her face and arms and hands, then her back and breasts and stomach, now her hair – my god, her hair! – shaking loose from a careful beehive, steadfast through thirty years of revolving page boys, Dorothy Hamill bobs, and Farrah Fawcett manes: that's how people knew Bobbie was Bobbie: a woman of steel, loyal to her beehive. But now Bobbie's cracking and peeling like the packaging on some flimsy substandard product she'd order only once then never again, saying politely but firmly over the phone, Please don't send me any more Puissance, Mr. Lederer; in addition, I will be returning my previous order of twelve. And after fifteen years of dealing with her Mr. Lederer would know enough to simply say, Yes, Mrs. Chernin, no more Puissance.

So Bobbie sucks in her stomach and looks straight ahead, almost as if Annette's not there. Oh, Bobbie says. Not too bad today, Annette. Not *too* bad.

Annette promises to stop by at five-thirty with a chunk of kolbassa for Bobbie to take home to Larry, part of a present from Stu to Annette.

Annette and Stu go back at least eleven years, to when Annette used to run the meat counter and she'd receive his great hulking carcasses on the loading platform, and it was no secret – not to Bobbie or to anyone else – that together Stu and Annette would inspect the order in the walk-in freezer.

For years, in fact, Bobbie used to stand in the staff washroom at six while Annette (that smile!) leaned her rear against the stainless-steel sink – and oh, that Stu: how he'd casually place his warm hand on the small of Annette's back and steer her between the whole hogs and the sides of beef gently swinging from the steel hooks and, as if they were taking a stroll through the park, Stu might say, By the way, Annette, I took your advice and thought some more about starting my own shop, and Annette would just smile and they'd walk and talk like that for a while.

(And holding her hands under the hand dryer in the staff washroom at six, Bobbie could imagine how Annette, standing in the shower that night – as Annette dragged a razor up the firm inside of her left leg, and then again after her shower, as she expertly worked cocoa-butter lotion into every inch of skin – how Annette might think of Stu and smile again; only this time her lips would stretch and part to expose her excellent teeth and, behind them, the pinky muscle of tongue, laced with white.)

But when Mr. Owens called Annette into his office one morning and said, Annette, we think a lady like you would be better off in Confections, Annette had been so defiantly angry (I *love* Meats, Mr. Owens) that – even though she'd served the blue-rinse set this and that, rung up their orders, wrapped their packages of pastel-coloured Choco-Pops for great-nieces and grand-nephews – Annette's eyes had remained dark and muddy from her runny mascara all day long.

I don't care any more, she'd told Bobbie in the staff washroom at noon.

So once a month now for seven years, Stu brings homemade kolbassa to the candy counter, carefully passing the lumpy package past the mountains of jelly beans, reaching up and out to Annette as she dishes out pepper-mint wafers and candied ginger behind the inviolable fortress of Sweet Delights.

At least, Bobbie thinks as she leaves Annette and continues left past the rows of men's briefs, at least Annette didn't have to give up her white food-staff coat and spend a mint like Bobbie does on clothes.

Bobbie's hands start to ache pretty bad as she turns the key in her cash register and Mary leaves for lunch. Bobbie hopes she won't be too busy, because Larry will drop by in half an hour to say hello, having closed his shoe store and taken the subway to skate for an hour at Nathan Phillips Square at lunch time. And as Larry's blades bite into the ice and he twirls forward and backward, *everyone* – executive secretaries in fox furs mingling reluctantly with skins and punks – will stop to watch, just like when Larry was in the Navy and he'd perform for the men on leave, his skinny hairy legs sticking out from a pink gingham dress with apron, his blonde wig and falsies silhouetted by the spotlight, Larry spinning faster and faster across the rink – his favourite role being Goldilocks, as chased by the three bears.

So Bobbie hopes she won't be too busy, because even though she and Larry don't talk much at the counter, still, they like to stand there a moment, not saying much, just looking at the people around them. After a silence, Bobbie will shift her weight to her right foot and resettle her bust on the counter. Then she'll say, Jean bought a new sofa yesterday. Green floral, six weeks delivery. In reply Larry will say, Health-food store next door's going out of business. Then Bobbie will spray him with this week's sample atomizer, and Larry will leave.

In fact, Larry's due in fifteen minutes now, so Bobbie's nervously eyeing the young guy lingering at Timothy E's across from her. She knows the type: he'll need a little Obsession to match the hundred-and-fifty-dollar casual-wear shirt that's probably in the bag from the Polo shop;

but first he'll make Bobbie take out and test every cologne she has to offer; she'll have to compare prices, sizes, possible side effects, clashing *colours* and *notes*; he'll say, But does the high note of Mood Indigo clash with the (barely visible) violet streaks on my new tie? and he'll take it from its box, pure silk and ninety-five at least, Bobbie thinks, bought from that new queer from Expressions on Three.

Bobbie waits. Before she leaves tonight she'll pick up three pairs of men's bikinis, thirty per cent off on top of her employee's discount. She thinks she'll get the white with royal-blue pinstripes – nautical, a little saucy, Larry's manly balls sitting in them nicely. Bobbie likes to think of Larry – her Larry – on the ice, twirling in a cloud of whatever cologne's on special: Larry whirling in a cloud of Aramis one week, Drakkar Noir the next.

Bobbie's hands prickle cold and she looks down at them, checking for new eruptions, and when she looks up the stylish young man who was shopping at Timothy E's stands in front of her.

Bobbie says, Can I help you? but he's not looking at her; instead, he's frowning and looking down.

And there, between them on the counter, lie numerous strands of Bobbie's hair, like rings inside a tree, one day circling one another like so many cracks and wrinkles, the fissures of her body endlessly repeating.

(Hygiene, Mr. Owens had said. Retirement, Bobbie.)

At night, Bobbie lies next to Larry. This has gone on forever, Bobbie thinks lately, lying in bed while she unpeels next to him, a barely audible loosening gentle as (what was once) his sweet breath between snores. Each thumping snore that used to wake her had resounded like applause and she'd whirl and twirl her way back down through the mists of sleep and every night had been the same, Larry landing perfectly, exactly where the spotlight shone, his blades throwing arabesques of ice high up into the volatile air only to explode around his shoulders and sparkle like sequins, and applause arced above his head, every night the same, Larry dipping and soaring across the vast ice and the sailors on leave clapping and cheering and as he leaps into the air for the double-axel and lands, poof, then sweeps backward in a figure-eight the crowd roars even louder – and Larry's snores at night had sounded just like that.

These nights, though, when Bobbie lies next to Larry, she can't sleep. She retires in two days now, and can't for the life of her figure out what that means. She knows she *loves* him (her strong feet still touch his once at three in the morning, twice at five); she's just nervous and confused.

She stares at the plastered-over spot on the ceiling and feels madder than hell, but she doesn't know why, really, only that the feeling's getting worse, and she's lost her appetite and dropped six pounds, and maybe she'll never sleep a wink again as long as she lives.

Things fall apart, Bobbie thinks, and her stare bores into the spot on the ceiling, and her rage just grows. Then slowly her breasts begin to rise higher and fall lower and her eyes start to roll back slightly in her head, then snap back again to the spot but with decreasing focus each time.

When Bobbie finally steps through that spot on the ceiling the music will be playing loud and bumpy, *ba-boom*, *ba-boom*, the lights fast-switching on and off, purple and yellow, the room bleary with reds and bilious greens and Bobbie will feel queasy, maybe she shouldn't have had that fourth Sling. It's like when Bobbie and the girls went to the Love Boat one night for their Christmas get-together, and they'd joked about what if Mr. Owens danced here, and each of the girls in turn had thrilled and gasped when Mr. Tease singled each of them out and smiled, and when he smiled at Bobbie in the packed bar that night – this man pulsing his groin in and out as the strobe light flashed, rolling his pelvis back and forth – light wisps of Bobbie's blonde hair floated free from her usually perfect coiffure, and Bobbie hadn't known or else she didn't even care, her hair wild and damp and free, Mr. Tease smiling, Bobbie and the girls laughing and hollering for more.

Only now it's Bobbie up there, clambering onto the stage, and nobody's more surprised than Bobbie (shouldn't have had that fifth Sling).

Stepping into the spotlight, she's nervous, a long white feather boa trailing from her shoulders while she's wiggling and peeling off these long white kidskin gloves and as she tugs at each skinny finger, every real and imagined kiss in Bobbie's life collides in the seductive *now* of her dream.

Bobbie's nervous, yes, but nervous as a newborn baby; she's restless, a little reckless, and she feels a million pounds lighter. Any moment now she'll be taking off.

Boris

Boris walks at night through our house. His face is green, sometimes emerald-green like a lizard's, but only when he's very hungry. I say, Don't go into the basement, and when my brother says, Why? I say, Just don't. My brother cries a little and my mother gets mad: *Big baby*. Then she says, You're scaring your brother. *Miss Smarty-pants*.

When Boris walks up the stairs he keeps his eyes shut tight, not because he's asleep – because he's dead.

The hallway's dark.

My brother and I sit tight, and the light from the TV scrapes our faces blue. The mad doctor laughs, and I try not to spill from the tray on my lap as I pass my brother his drink. When the doctor laughs again my brother and I press our heads to the back of the couch.

There's a boy who plays at the edge of the woods. All by himself. A crowd gathers in town. They shout, wave torches. I'm letting my brother eat Cheerios and he sucks each mouthful to a soft whine, and his pyjamas crisp nice against my shoulder.

The air crackles and pops, blue and white explosions.

The boy looks up. Stumbles, faints.

When something drags him deep into the woods the doctor laughs and laughs and I hold the tray tight as men and women scream, mouths cracked into surprise.

I stop chewing, mouth full of crumble.

Listen, I tell my brother, and I nod toward the hallway. It's Boris. Can't you hear him?

The TV spits fire, spits lightning and I can see my brother's face – how he just *looks*.

I lean closer.

March march march, I say, and I tell him how my ears pound against my head.

I told my brother something. Last Saturday afternoon in the parking lot at the grocery store. My mother parked the car. Got out, leaned back inside. Looked me hard in the eye.

When a strange man knocks on the door don't let him in. Don't let your brother out.

She left and I rolled the car windows up tight. I locked the doors shut. I counted *wait-wait*, tick-tock like a clock. Said, sharp as scissors, Don't move.

He kicked the seat in front of him, testing. We'd played

this before: the steering wheel a throat, the dashboard alive with tortures.

I clicked and growled.

I said, Believe me.

Air still as cliffs, like waiting for something to start or to stop – slip over the waiting, fall all the way forward.

Then there's only my brother, sitting still in the car like he's frozen. But I'm still saying, It'll get you – I don't stop.

And after a while I do.

Then my brother and I wait quietly in the car for my mother. Seems like forever. And in the summer forever's very hot. In the winter it's very cold.

I think Boris's heart is like that, misery thickened to heavy machinery that turns and turns and inside its cold parts (somewhere *in there*) I can hear my own voice.

The TV gurgles now, it hisses. Boris walks.

After the first movie. After the crackers and toast. After the first half of the second movie, when my brother falls asleep, and I wake him.

Bed, I say.

I take him down the hallway to his room. I put the covers over him and he's so sleepy, tomorrow he won't remember how he got there.

From the hallway I can see the TV flash and fade, and I don't look down the stairs. When I go back into the room and turn off the TV it smokes to grey then dies to black.

I lie in my bed.

All night long, Boris.

His arms stretch in front of him and his hands open and shut, open and shut, very slowly, and they're white with wormy grey veins, and his hands are very strong, and cold. When I pee the bed it's hot and the hotness makes my legs warm.

But then the pee grows cold, and smells bad, and I know my mother will yell in the morning.

You could never stop him. This is something I know, and I don't know if my brother knows it, but I do, and that's all that matters.

So I never even try.

What my brother and I know for sure is this: there are bad people. We're not so sure about good people.

Bela.

My brother and I hold hands above the vampire. Close our eyes.

Bel-ah.

Chase each other over the bed, under the bed. Tear around the wastepaper basket until I bang into it – blue, green, yellow construction paper spews out, and we trample it and yell at each other, we yell at the top of our lungs – I vant to suck your blood – until our mother shouts up the stairs.

You kids'll be the death of me.

Bela's cape looks like my father's best tweed jacket. My brother picked the cape up before the paint dried, finger-prints on the black outside and on the red inside. Okay. Bela's an *English* vampire who roams the moors by night. Very polite when he greets his guests at Buckingham.

Good eve-eh-ning.

Step right this way, over here we have the famous Creature, the Creature from the Black Lagoon. The hardest to put together. First we lost his spiny tail. A star of claws went next. We take him out of the box and lay him on the floor and small bits of plastic surround him like a magic circle. Kick some away, by accident, and they're like a trail of crumbs, and we can follow them to the Creature's wandering tail.

My brother says, When.

Supper's ready. You kids get down here now.

Boris. Nothing's missing. His skin shines dull as a dead man's. Pants tattered, black like the black knobs on each side of his head. Only I can place him back in his box to rest, wrapped in green tissue paper and bits of silver tinsel left over from last Christmas.

Handle with care! Disease! Injury!

My brother's still wondering about the Creature.

It's fun knowing more than someone else.

•

She'll have to go upstairs and clean up after us. She knows it. Fish sticks. Coke and canned peaches. She says she's the Shit-Lady, and all we ever do is shit on her. That's all people'll ever do to you. You and your so-called friends. (Listen to the mouth on her, my father says.)

After supper my brother and I go outside. We split a Vachon cake. In the morning dragonflies ride double in the ditch and the grass fattens damp under your feet. But at seven o'clock the trees darken to fists and the birds cry loud and long and you can look for them as long as you like and never see one at all.

We turn the corner from Hillcrest Crescent onto Princess Street. It's almost summer-warm. The fall leaves rot sweet into my nose.

That's where Wendy fell off her bike when the chain grabbed her foot and she tried to turn the handlebars but the gravel jerked her tires. Off she went – ten feet at least straight through the air and into the ditch, and her skirt flew around her head. (When I told my father, he wanted to know, Could you see her bare arse? Yes, you could, I said. You could see her bare arse.)

And yesterday I went looking, and I found a yellow

streamer from Wendy's handlebars, wrapped tight around a rock in the ditch, but I never gave it back.

Underwear, the bare tops of Wendy's legs. Arse.

I didn't use to know how to ride a bike. My cousin Ruth showed me. We were at her house by the lake. Uncle Roy fell asleep on the floor, after my father took my mother and Ruth's mother shopping. Uncle Roy drinks. Like candy to a baby, my mother says. My father says, Imagine, a grown man. My mother says, What do you expect. Mumma spoiled him.

Ruth and I went outside. We had purple licorice strings, to tie together or braid, and foamy powder kegs that fizz up your nose when you suck the licorice wick. She took me behind her house (shack, my father calls it) and I found a frog. Ruth said, No, it's a toad.

The lake shone blue. My nose hurt.

Ruth said, Come over here. Hurry. But there were nails everywhere (junk, junk heap) so I had to go slow. Big boards, rusted metal growing up like grass.

She stood beside the tool shed, holding two corners of a big dirty sheet, as high as my waist, higher, lumpy, orange-brown. Dirty water and dead bugs caught in its folds.

Abracadabra.

A hush like wings flapping. And then from the house a door slammed, and my cousin Ruth had that big orange sheet only halfway up. Breeze catching at the edges – and I froze, too.

My father calling to me. He must have left our mothers in town. They drive him crazy, two old broads.

We could hear him, kicking the garbage can by the steps. Calling me. Saying, Little bitch, when I didn't answer.

I looked at Ruth. Pull it off, I thought. Pull it. And when my father called again I thought, Don't.

A door slammed a second time, and the house was quiet. She pulled off the cover. Her new bike shone blue, like it'd been skimmed off the top of the lake. We didn't say anything for a moment.

Nice bike.

She said, Ride it!

So I did, straight down the path behind the house and into the woods, and the lake flashed like coins through slots of trees, silver, silver-blue, silver and the blue of the bike high above the lake.

I rode that bike fast – and what Ruthie told everybody later was wrong, I rode it really far, then I stopped. And lying between rocks and roots on the path, I could see the blood on my knee was even brighter than Ruthie's bike.

My brother and I check the ditch on Princess Street again. Nothing there, so we climb back out. I can see Wendy and her older sister Marie, but they're far off, at least halfway up the street and close to Willowdale Avenue where the cars all go.

Wendy and Marie are talking to Kathy Martin, who's taller than Marie, taller than even the boys in the Grade Five class at school. Their shorts dust to grey in the twilight. I want to catch up, but the stones from the side of Princess Street catch in the backs of my flip-flops, and each time I stop to shake the stones out my brother says, Rather we go home.

Four-year-old in blue seersucker pyjamas and a straw tourist-hat from Mexico, fringed with red pompoms. *Rather* he do this, *Rather* that.

Know-it-all, my mother says to me sometimes. My brother's face a tight hard rock that won't budge. His big words make me angry because now it's him, not me, who thinks he knows.

The street lights are still off. I want to see them come on, all at once. But all I see are the twirly bats as they fall through the near-dark around us.

When I get to 224 Princess Street I stop. He's ten steps behind me so I turn around and wait. Dark green curtains in the window, full of shadow. Wrought-iron railing up the dark brown steps. Cracked. Steep. Even the untrimmed shrubs that line the long drive.

He catches up.

Look.

But he can't, he's so scared he runs and it's funny, how his arms and legs jerk in different directions at once like they might snap right off.

I pass the house. Curtains move.

(I'm sure.)

Run.

In Kathy Martin's kitchen the spoons go somewhere else.

I hold one in my hand and reach up and pull open the white drawer, but only halfway. Kathy Martin laughs and says, It always sticks. Reaches down and pulls it open for me.

Wendy and her older sister Marie wipe the pots and pans.

Nobody turns the kitchen light on so the street light from Willowdale Avenue shines in the window. Kathy Martin opens the fridge door. That light shines too.

I think I hear a bus go by. Not sure, so I don't say.

When I look inside the drawer I look hard at the tray but I can only see forks where my mother would put the spoons. I can see plastic corn cobs at the bottom of the tray, and I don't even know what they're for.

My brother sits in a chair in the corner. I can't see him too well. He has his hat on, and he's quiet. Looking around, swinging his legs.

Nobody tells him to stop.

I look harder at the tray. She could take the spoon-drying away from me.

My brother's laughing. Kathy gives him a Popsicle. But to Wendy and Marie and me she only gives tall glasses of water.

Then Kathy Martin says, Spoons over there, and points to the left of the knives.

I drop my spoon in, dry two more.

When Kathy Martin's father comes into the kitchen he turns the light on. He looks like my father asleep, face twisted swollen like a balloon the day after it's pumped up. Air shrinking inside.

At first Kathy Martin's father just looks at us. He's been sleeping. His chest is hairy and his underwear bags loose around his legs. He bangs his fist down on the counter and the still-dirty dishes bounce up and clink. Rubs his hands over his face. Walks over to the table and pulls out a chair, slowly tilts it back. He makes a noise and I think he's saying something, but Kathy Martin and Marie hold on to their glasses and don't say a word, so I can't really tell.

Oh.

My brother's Popsicle melts cherry-red down his arm. Sticky. He doesn't notice.

I'm not going to clean it up, I don't care.

Wendy starts to hiccup, she always does when she's scared – she can't stop. I think, Shut up. Please. Then Kathy Martin's father says, Jesus, very slowly. Jee-sus. And he lets the chair fall.

Fuckers, he says. Get the fuck home.

And once, my mother came into my room late at night. This is something I never tell.

Wake up. We're leaving.

She dressed me, but she forgot one sock, and I liked how my bare foot felt inside my boot – strange. Like someone else's foot.

My heel rubbing against the felt liner.

We walked to the park on Spring Garden Avenue. She talked fast. Words I couldn't put together, and by themselves they didn't make sense.

Brown gloved hand on my arm. She brushed my hair out of my eyes.

The lights from the houses on the street above the park looked warm. She was laughing. Saying things like, Oh, and the time, then laughing before she finished talking and holding my hand and jerking it when she got excited.

Then she laughed and rode the slide, even though it was wet with snow. I watched to make sure she didn't slip backward and bump her head, the way she sometimes did for my brother and me. After the slide she wanted to ride the teeter-totter, so I sat on the opposite end from her and she laughed as she jerked me into the air.

At first I laughed, too. And then I didn't – riding high up and the houses on the street above us silent and frozen.

And I held on tight because I thought I might fall, squeezed hard against the giant arc of rusted metal creaking like a breath held up or down on the in or out, all that still cold air turning inside me.

My eyes watered hard against the sharp night – I knew there was no one to catch me. Until up that high all I could see were the black spaces between the up and down swing of blue and red metal, the houses just blurs of light.

A blurry star moving at the top of the hill.

My mother stopped.

We walked up the hill and got into the car. My father drove us home. She was quiet. He said, Don't tell your friends about your crazy mother.

I'm eight. I'm ten. I'm twelve.

Sometimes I don't think about much, being older, and the old games so stupid. I go out with my friends. My brother stays in his room and adds this to that with his chemistry set. Test tubes foam, surge with secret formulas. Break. Guess he doesn't know much, like how to put the parts together.

Snap, snap crackle pop.

And sometimes. Boris only a dream at night, foggy, a man in my room. Sitting in a chair. Go back to sleep, he says. He moves his hands over my legs, is it cold. Can I run. Maybe it's hot.

My father always says, Go back to sleep.

And there was that time once, at the end of Princess Street, before you turn onto Hillcrest Crescent and walk the three doors to our house, when I stopped running and turned around.

I can see him up the road, moving through the dark between the street lights toward me. He's lost his Mexican hat, and as he gets closer I can see his mouth snap open and shut, open and shut. Very fast.

I can't hear a thing.

Or I hear something, like something's spinning or chug-chugging only it's not my brother and it's not me, or is it.

And coming up to me like that on Princess Street his face looked funny. All surprised and jangly, like he was all beaten up inside. He was crying, and I hit him and hit him, we were so afraid, and I was so mad.

And that's what it was like, being young and having a little brother – just no good people, maybe. And a Creamsicle, or maybe a chocolate float.

You eat it fast. You try not to make a mess.

··

I Do Things

Fat man – so hard to move around – likes to lie on his back on my bed. I do things to him. He touches soft. He cries sad sometimes, small noises, very nice to hear.

Fat man, soft man – the things he's whispered into me! *Suck me, precious, suck me* – and it's soft and small, such a little thing.

First, I begin to work at home. I find I like to get out on weeknights and weekends. But when we go to a movie it's like he's so fat I don't know him, just know how fat he is – standing in front of or behind me, not talking, in the lineup that stretches into the mall – and I notice how people look at him after he's bought our tickets and moves upstairs to the bathroom (and this is hard for him to do, he breathes very hard doing this).

I think, What would it be like to stand next to him at a urinal? I wouldn't breathe a word.

Sometimes I wait in the lobby until he's sitting in the theatre. I enter and walk to the opposite side of the aisle, and I make the whole row stand for me, and I sit down beside him.

In the darkened theatre, over the red plush seats, the king and queen bow – ah, splendid together, flattened to the screen. Trumpets announce their departure. In a faraway land a hundred horses enter the skirmish, the plains are swept with glory.

Red string licorice, and popcorn. Popcorn.

And out of the whirl, the dust-arcs of valour, the avenging knight, his armour a shape hinging form to form and the mounting tension, the almost unbearable excitement as he forays, clack-clack, further in his quest. The queen waits in her glory robes, her modest room lit from a small window high above her head, her narrow cot untouched. They've both travelled far, their shining raiments torn.

We pass a drink between us, drinking from the same straw until the drink's finished. Then we have another.

And once, outside on the sidewalk, I took his hand. Because I'm nice to him. I treat him nice.

He calls me, *Small slip of a thing, tip of the tongue.*

Clothes cost so much. He says he needs something to cover his butt, size 56, 60, 64. He swells. I sit in the chair outside the men's dressing room. The sales help barely acknowledge me. Soon he exhausts the bargain bins at the Bay, where I've watched him root excitedly for shorts, pants, shirts. In the Mr. Big 'n Tall he examines suits. I've never seen so much brown. He picks out a pair of pants and shows me the fly: cheap plastic he'll take to the dry cleaners to have replaced with a durable metal one. I follow him, finger broadcloth, polyblend. I linger at midnight blue, single-breasted. *This is nice*, I say. But he's gone, I can barely see him. Over by the shirt racks. Now by the socks. He selects a belt and moves to the cash register.

He says, *That'll be cash.*

I stand in the middle of the aisle, between the crowded racks of coats and shelves of extra-large sweaters, and I can see everything here costs so much. *This is terrible*, I say, because these are the important things in his life. I look around me, mutter about cheap flies.

Later, we stop for lunch. He says, *You don't know what it's like.*

I shift in my oversized coat. He tells me I'm nothing if not thin.

Sometimes – I dance with him. This happens late at night, after the news and before we go to bed. The radio plays in the kitchen. I don't know the steps so I follow, and we move slow as statues across the checkerboard floor. I think of terrazzos and breezes under the stony vault of night, the tap tap of my ball-gowned surrender, right foot, left foot and the shadow as my skirt arcs from one tiled square to another.

Sometimes, in the evening, we play chess and I out-smart him, queen to rook to pawn. He outsmarts me, his dark knight slices across the board. Queen to knight to queen. Our peregrinations never seem to end.

Sometimes I lie on my side – with my stomach against his back, my arm around his heaving shoulder. Sleeping. (Some of the things I can barely endure: sleep, sheep, the clock radio red, alert as eyes, ears, every second that counts begins to squeeze me against the wall: all the other nights, too – I couldn't sleep, turn over, move a muscle, breathe against him pressed to me until I breathed his air into me and it filled me up and kept me going until morning. That was until I learned to take my pills, same shape, size, all these little pills – learned to take them, to sleep.)

Today he calls me from work. What did he have for lunch? He breathes very soft in my ear. *Excuse me*, he says. *Bob. Yeah. I got her up and running. Sorry*, he says. *What were you saying?* I hold the paper bag I've been breathing into close. *Are you there?* he says. I nod, look at the bag, its brown creases. Pop, I think. Pop.

And later, when we're washing dishes after dinner, he says, *You are closer to me than family – family always lets you down.* Then he takes the soapy glass from me, and wipes it. Spoon, pan. I scrape the bowl, then leave it to soak. He dries two forks, and puts them in the drawer. He says, *Precious, my precious.* I push the dish rack under the sink. And now the kettle boils and boils but I'm not going to make a move – his hand on my hip, his voice in my ear.

Turn it off, I say, finally.

Tonight he says, *Please, mommy, please,* and, *No, mommy, no.* And I am thin, pressing down hard. He's a big boy. When I lie on top of him his breasts move clammy-grey beneath me.

I shock him sometimes, I say shocking things but I can safely say this: that love thins to no substitute, only love can fill you, make you do these things behind closed doors once they've clacked shut – that only love can let you inside and leave you there, together alone. Turn to each other: lovely.

I've rattled around his big body many times now, and I wonder what it would be like to be big, too, but I can't think about it for long – my thin spine like a line attached and running through us while I'm thin, thin, thin on his big body, fast and amazing, a crawly thing, clack-clack and it's done, amazing, the things I do.

Aerodrome

Your wife looks good in white slacks – she always has. She cuts Mrs. Connor's hair in your home, dark sprinkles on your wife's slim legs. You look through the sliding-glass door. Your wife works fast, her scissors precise as parabolas through the air-conditioned room. She's professional. The garden hose is a mess, how did that happen, you take such care. You untangle it. Not a breath of air in the damp August heat, muggy as blankets. Inside, your wife tilts Mrs. Connor's head forward, combs the hair out. You like that your wife works at home. Her hands are cool against the cheek when she cuts your hair, thin and brown in her light hands. You spray the beets. The sweet peas climb. Mrs. Connor's mouth moves, she laughs, waves her hands under her apron but your wife is silent, she steps back when Mrs. Connor laughs loud, your wife checks her work like you'd put up a wall and check it, perfect plumb.

The string beans uncoil.

It's been a bad summer. The old collie (your boy and girl grew up with him!) had to be put down. Bastard flies settled on a hot spot where the dog licked and licked: eggs lodged inside his back right leg, the vet said, beneath the long black coat where they were hard to see.

And when you did – when Prince started to limp and you had to know why – too late.

You didn't know such things could happen.

You finish in the garden, lean your head against the shovel's handle. What can you do, already August, lettuce next, no, you don't know what, aphids sour against the grass, the zucchini huge, too huge to eat.

You take long showers, sharp needles until the hot water runs out. Outside, the tomatoes ascend, bulge like flatus through the moist afternoon. You weren't always like this.

Try to think what's happened.

You shake your head slowly under the shower, stitches of cold water – a big man gone sodden though cold water battens down the hatches.

On Saturdays you load the van and drive to the flea-market on the 400. The gewgaws aren't selling well. This has happened gradually, so that at first you didn't notice. Hard, sometimes, to see the whole for the parts. You should know, first-class mechanic once, before they screwed you over at the shop.

You could fix anything.

What else.

The boy got his pilot's licence in May.

To celebrate, you take him to Kelsey's for dinner. (The girl won't come; the wife is working.) You order the ribs, sticky sweet. You tell the boy he'll like them, though you don't think he'll even notice, he's so excited at getting his licence, his words – *fuselage, atmospheric pressure* – trailing him like jet exhaust in a soar to eight thousand even when, after dinner, the ribs lie vanquished before you, your napkin crumpled and grease-stained.

Finished. You're finished.

The boy buzzes and hums, you can't stop him. Makes you tired.

The waiter comes and you rally. Smile winningly: you know what you want, you're sure and decisive, that's always been your strength, to know what's needed, to draw on your reserve. To never surrender.

Wave your hand.

Waiter, bring two, please.

The boy glares: got him now, clipped his wings a little, he banks both hands palm down on the table, trades altitude for speed, begins the tailspin to maximum urge – really, he's just like you! chief aerialist, never-say-die dogfighter – to thrust down (finally down) into the twin walls of trifle the waiter sets before you (mind you, not good English trifle, short on the sherry, perhaps, the cream synthetic, not fresh like the wife makes it, but really – what can you do?).

The boy has stopped talking. He won't look at you.

Your children, it seems, never miss a trick, never forgive. You like this trait. Say to the boy (grin like mad), Remember Buttonville?

You loved those family outings (though they happened years ago); everything in its proper place, wife and children, and you showing them what there was to see, for example the airplanes at Buttonville Airport – yes, the planes were your favourite, even on a cold Sunday morning and you can't deny the boy's current interest carefully cultivated by you.

Come on. You don't want to see those rubbishy lions, flea-bitten sorry things.

(Besides, the African Safari Game Farm was so far away.)

Come on. Your old dad knows what you like.

And it was true. Beneath the vertical snap of the windsock the boy and girl scuttled madcap, arms capering at their sides like planes' wings in a turbulent sky, Piper Cubs, Cessnas perched beside the hangar like sharp insects but common, all common, you'd noted with disdain to your wife, the boy and girl looking up at you with round blank faces because you – formerly Third Regiment RAF, Channel Dash veteran – could tell them so much.

Your wife pouring your tea from the Thermos and handing you the cup.

The vintage Beechcraft Staggerwing by the hangar attracting your attention.

The boy and girl sputter like Tiger Moths in the long glare of tarmac, and in the wind you can barely hear their skittish voices. You have to shout to make them hear you, to make them stop and behave.

Stop it now.

Stop.

When they look back at you their faces are ruddy with wind, their voices retreat as if sucked back to wind-tunnel throats by negative velocity – your children skid wild as atoms, small matter. You run to them, calling stop, the Staggerwing rising against the light-grey tarmac flattened by the bright April sun to rectangles against the brown field, the Staggerwing attracting you madly, madly.

Your wife crying – Leave them alone, she says, her arms raised, elbows knocking.

Stop, or I'll slap *you* silly too.

And you, huge as wind-shear, ate air as you stood on that field wide as the tiger-lily sky over wartime Malta, your Gladiator a flaming blossom of plane.

The boy remembers (he pushes his plate away) – oh, he never forgets – and you like that, too.

The waiter brings more coffee. The boy won't touch the stuff, says it's bad for the nerves. Good for him.

You have to go to the bathroom. Stand up, cuff the boy. Everyone can see you're close.

In the bathroom you think about your gewgaws: plastic bartaps with horsey scenes on them. Used to be popular in rec rooms – what's wrong with them now?

Rack your brains.

All summer you take long drives on Sunday mornings to meet your flying club at the field near Shelburne. (The girl won't come, you gave up long ago trying to interest her. God knows where she goes, what she does so beyond you. Your wife says leave the girl alone.) Together, you and the boy help hitch sailplanes to Jeeps. When it's your turn to fly you hang quiet as a bird, chaste as the air – long altimetered minutes on the cool lift of airflow on metal that leans clean into nothing but above and below, nothing but that.

Calms you to think of it.

You think it was early June. On the gliding field, your wife holds her drink. Ben stands close to her. You've all known each other a long time. Your wife says something to him, the weather May-cool and bright. She wears a

jacket, jade-coloured, and the girl's white sweatpants –
and you know how they fit your wife! as, up here the sky
unzipped to thermal nothing, you can imagine what Ben
sees when he looks at her. You ascend until the sky leans
clean through the top of your head, sun silvering the wind
to razors – and you drop a thousand feet, your eyes
spilling afternoon sky to the ground.

You think they meet in the Burger Shack.

You bet they hold hands across the table. Their fries
dissolve in vinegar, the tang inches down their throats.

You think one day you're going to push the door open.
The air conditioner will buzz steady as the rain-swollen
skies of August – that's how you'll think of it, click, the
gunmetal grey of sky.

A bad summer. You stand in the garden for hours,
pyjamas limp along your legs, damp at the waist. The
earthworms churn beneath your pale soft feet. In the heat
the zucchini explodes, yellow-white on the lawn.

Meanwhile your wife's scissors part the air as she holds
to her cool geometry. She knows what she's doing and
you like that.

Your wife has long white fingers. She calls you inside.
She's finished cutting Mrs. Connor's hair – your wife tells

you she's finished. She's dressed in white, tiny speckles of dark, and you like to look at her when she gets up from the table and leaves the room.

Your daughter, your lesbian daughter – imagine all that's happened to you – this girl, teenager, young lady, shakes her head in disgust.

Even the boy – he turns his head when you reach up over the dinner table to pluck a fly from thin air, prize, petal, medal, Bloody damn bastards, you shout, Bastards. You're thinking of poor old Prince (Prince! – the boy and girl grew up with him).

There's more.

The whole *Regia Aeronautica* at Valetta and your blood pressure rising like a plane.

Prince!

Your fat head buzzing nine weeks in hospital, and still those nerves wouldn't cure.

Couldn't have, because you hear it again *up* like when the whole side of your head shook – thick sky above and no below – and you, red with the angry rasp of your plane, shook the enemy air to earth.

Oh, it's this whole bastard head that buzzes.

. . . .

Driving Men Mad (Scheherazade)

Tell me something, he says.

We have clematis. Alyssum. At one we nap. Drinks at three. Her bathing suit is pink. Pink splash borders the pool.

He doesn't laugh.

We have a white porch, a swing. A ghost called Lady Jamais, famous on the island. Nights calling in the garden, voice soft as water from the sprinklers beneath the grass.

I say, I'm making this up as I go along.

Dogwood leaps, tongue and stem. I admire his arms. His smooth skin.

Lean against me, I say.

She hooks a finger, two, a fist into me. Shouts, Bitch. You goddamned bitch.

She's got these big eyes.

We've been together a long time. We're in love.

A woman lies on another woman. Lies and lies. A woman. A man. A woman. Nothing I say can make it any better.

Tell me about yourself, he says.

All those Pre-Raphaelites pored over, first menstruation and its lusts. We thought we were alone. We thought there were gardens. We thought there was a ghost, un-requited lovers, we made one up and called her Lady Jamais, death-burred, tragic as stars, tongue studded with sinking moons.

I obsess over her breasts. Hips. Till death us do part. Teenage girls are like this, better believe it. It is always a matter of life and death.

I visit her on the ninth floor, nomenclature of girl suicides: Ninth floor, please, psychiatric. At the nurses' station we ask permission to go to the cafeteria, where we load up on tiny bags of bite-sized Oreos, man, we work that vending machine as if playing pinball. She tells me she hides her pills under her tongue. Swallows fast. This is the kind of girl I really go for. Of course she's upbeat, you'd be too if you scarfed down a couple hundred of your mother's best Ativan, the happy drug of choice.

Make an effort, the nurses exhorted yesterday when she refused to attend the group session. Sounds like a bowel movement, she told them.

Bam-smang goes the cafeteria vending machine. Five bags, six bags. We've got five minutes left. Or else, the nurse had said.

We run out of quarters. We wait for the elevator with a bunch of old sick people. We take the stairs instead.

You're late, a nurse says.

I leave in the elevator. I'm carrying all these little bags. Do I toss them. Do I eat them and gain, like, a million pounds. I stand in the lobby. Life, I deduce, is complicated. Things will always, will only, get worse.

Not like this guy, I think, years later. He's simple. I lay him over and over. He's in shock, astonishment leaks from his fingertips, his toes when I rub him down.

Then eat him alive.

It's not like he has much money. None of us do. Money might make it easier. To go to Greece and fuck like mongrels. A scene of contrition in the Luxembourg Gardens. God, what I wouldn't give for a weekend in Winnipeg.

What he and I do instead is this: meet halfway, in Thunder Bay. The room's cold. We attract stares from locals. We're brave, we hold on to each other, drunk. I like your arms, I tell him in the lumpy bed.

He says, I like you too.

·

Tell me something, he says. We're on a bus. I hold my breath. Exhale. Pet dogs? Birthday parties? Other men. He's nervous asking about the women. What he really wants to know is so ordinary: does he stack up? I suspect he's jealous. I begin to credit him with being human. I am unspeakably cruel.

Tell me something.

In bed at his place I explete into his mouth. Nothing random in this: I shoot, I score. He's happy as a clam. He says he likes to finger fuck me. God, how many times do I have to tell him? Women *don't*, I say. They just fuck. Ah, his hand on my stomach. I can tell I'm not getting through. Women *fuck*, I say. He taps his index finger. Guys are too stupid sometimes. I do it – I use the *P-word*.

Phallocentric.

He rises on an elbow. He leans over me, he's hardly got any chest hairs, christ, I'm hairier than he is, I think. He blows me a kiss.

I flip him the finger. Jerk.

I begin to suspect him of hidden depths.

You're losing your culture, she says. You're past the point. You're so far beyond. There's no telling what you'll do next.

I think, My life. It's like every *Gunsmoke* rerun I've ever seen.

We make up. She takes me dancing at Wild Bill's. A lesbian cultural evening. We two-step the night away. George Strait sings "All My Exes Live In Texas." She leads, we do an inside turn, one two three, five. We do the Cowboy Hustle, we do Slap Leather. I get confused, screw up the Grapevine. I sit down, finish an Ex. I watch her. She's good, women like dancing with her. Especially the straight feminists, her friends from the Crisis Line. Especially Barbara Ann, who won't let her go for four songs. Especially Jill, who finally cuts in. Hips. Pretty face. Quite the gal, I tell her in the washroom. Through the double doors and into the cubicle where I do up my jeans I hear Patty Loveless sing "Jealous Bone." She sings along, waiting for me by the sink. I slap open the cubicle door. Goddamn straight women, I say.

She says she too wants to sleep with a man. She's woken me up, the street light bleeds through the window. Give me some covers, I say. It's been ten years, she says. She says, I can drive men mad, I used to. I say, I know. I know.

She's asleep. I get up, get a glass of water. What will she think of next?

I come back to bed. The covers are on the floor. I leave them there, all night. In the morning her back is warm against my breasts.

She meets him at a playwrights' conference. In Alberta. He's an alcoholic Newfie fag (I think), and he reads the part of a woman – brilliantly, she tells me, later. She has two vaginal orgasms with him, not clitoral, she says, knowing the distinction never fails to escape me. He beats off. He moans, I love you. That's what I think he said, she tells me. We laugh. She watches me carefully, for days.

I smell him on me sometimes. Sweat him, unavoidable. He's really there, I can't wipe him off, on my fingers, the sharp hairs of my legs.

One day we're walking to Mac's Milk.

We walk past Mr. Benjamin's shrubbery. Mr. Benjamin waves. What a nice day! On the other side of the street a woman in white shorts walks a Bouvier. We've seen her before, but not a lot, she's new to his neighbourhood. We agree we like Bouviers. We have so much in common. There's Mrs. Mathilde, home from Cuba. Hot, she says. Cuba was hot. What a nice day! He says, Love me. I say, I won't. We stop in front of Mac's, neither of us reaches for the door handle. He says, So tell me something new.

He cries when he comes.

Once, when we're having sex, he mishears me say, I need you.

Of course on the home front things go from bad to worse. The stays of her bodice, her long silvery plaits of hair, undone. Oh god I'm going to get it now.

She is spools and hooks of her weak heart, her chest pains. She kisses my ear. I haven't got long, she says. I refuse to be threatened. I refuse to get close. She tongues fricatives into me. I'm afraid because I have no words for this.

It's bad, I think. I can't stop the lies.

I marry him; there are no children. I move back to the island with her; I never leave.

What do you want me to do? she says.

I've always liked how she smokes, even though I don't myself indulge. She's smoking now, white cigarette she holds lightly in her long beautiful fingers. She smokes strong, with emphasis. She's always scared me a little. She inhales. Taps the ash into the blue ashtray. The geraniums are doing fine. Exhales: I've always found it sexy, wanted to kiss it from her, like steam, I imagine. Nice lips. I like your lips, I say. It's not working, I won't get off this easy, not now. Nope. It's Ultimatum Time. The poplar whirs. Her eyes a muddy blue. I smile inappropriately, simpleton. I squirm, she makes me feel small. I, um, like your lips, I want to say. I want to say. Smoke rises and roils. Rises and rises. Forsythia flickers in the breeze and glows. What do you want me to do.

It's bad when the story repeats too often. When they get tired of the lies. When there's nothing more to be said. Off with her head! And look: Lady Jamais, headless in the garden. A flicker. A longing of sweet basil, summer savoury powders the night air, words you can't hear but want to as she slips through the trees and into the swimming pool. She is the way roses look at night, bled of colour. She will never leave. This garden will flourish. She will slip past the cherry tree and into the sky. Fall down in a shower of star-dust. Rhododendrons applaud. Impatiens, their fierce pink, spread.

I can do this, I think, I can go on and on, who's to stop me?

Oh yeah, he says. I've heard that one before.

(Girls' Own) Horse Stories

The most embarrassing moment in her life.

At the track. Exercising a wired two-year-old with legs-for-days in front of the horse's investors. Just past the quarter-mile she realizes her sanitary napkin has bust loose and is booting it backward between her legs with each pounding beat. She's coming in to the home stretch now in front of the big shots and she's praying Dear lord in heaven don't let me don't let me lose it.

I'm going back to tampons, she announces to Louise during dinner that night. Let toxic shock take me.

Louise almost dies laughing. Almost.

Black Beauty. Ginger. Coco. Buckskin. Midnight. Hoot-Owl. Palomino-Pal-o'-Mine. Stalwarts bedding down for the night, having crossed the crooked stream, the mountain path by day. Benjy. Liebling-My-Love. Hey Dude.

Ariel, Sergeant, Big Bay: ten cents a ride at the Dominion store. She's tall in the saddle, the plastic mount cantering back and forth, back and forth.

This is the finest moment of my life, she thinks, age ten, riding home in Mrs. Taylor's Mustang, clutching an orange Honeydew and a hot dog from the grocery store snackbar.

National Velvet. My Friend Flicka.

That girl's horse-crazy.

Mrs. Taylor is too old to knock before she enters through the kitchen door. The old woman snorts and tosses her frizzy dyed hair. Mrs. Taylor's got pep.

She'll grow out of it, her mom says hopefully.

Mrs. Taylor smells of powder and nail polish.

Mrs. Taylor's hair, fine as a feathered fetlock.

Chestnut.

Hanoverians. Trakehners. She has a crush on Christilot Boylen, who wins the Bronze for dressage in the '76 Olympics. Oh beautiful, the commentator gushes. Look at that control!

She imagines cleaning tack together: lathering martingales, polishing spurs and stirrups. They take to the ring. Oh exquisite *passage*! Their habits chaste, alluring. Layers float then fall like apple blossoms. Lips meet once. Then it's round and round the ring again, flying lead changes everywhere. It's like slo-mo on CTV Sports. It's like love.

•

By the end of their first week as roommates in the apartment above the tack shed, she and Louise get along fine.

They watch John Wilsey turn out Bare Breeze – worth a lot of bananas, sperm $15,000 a pop – in Northwind's west pasture. John Wilsey has the metal chain of the lead shank across the stallion's upper gums for control. Looks like Mr. Ed's grumpy today. The horse shies at a puddle on the driveway: for two mil you get shit for brains. John Wilsey better rip his lips, she sure would, though only guys look after the studs. Bare Breeze side-slithers two steps then bunny hops the remaining four yards to the pasture gate, bouncing John Wilsey up and down in the mud like a ball.

She and Louise muck out the yearlings.

She raises the pitchfork. Stops and looks up: two down, twenty-eight baby Mr. Eds to go. Louise pushes the wheelbarrow over. Louise is strong for her size. Twenty-seven, twenty-six stalls left. A horse is a horse – she walks across the aisle to Louise – of course, of course. She knocks a wisp of straw from Louise's hair. Mr. Ed times thirty nickers softly. Louise puts the wheelbarrow down.

She believes this to be the strangest moment of her life.

The rape of brood mares. Three men holding the dam, two others assisting the stud, poor dumb fuck cock eighteen inches long four inches thick. He's so excited the whites of his eyes are tapioca and the men have to help him find the right hole. Yeah, they say. And more. She probably would too. She slams the apple juice into the grocery cart. Oh fucking right, Louise. You're always fucking right. Her Firebird a junk-bucket but it goes, stereo cranked and sparkling. She knows how it's done.

Lying in bed late at night, *Flipper* reruns on TV. Drunk enough (just enough), she imagines she's on that track again, a big dumb two-year-old beneath her. She's riding short, and it's like the first time because she's scared, bum barely grazing leather with every beat. She can feel the sanitary napkin bunching up, it must be halfway out of her jeans by now but she doesn't care, let the sucker fly. Black Beauty, Ginger, Coco. Benjy!

Cooling down, she drops the sweaty reins over the slackened neck. Leans back, pats the steaming flanks. When she was a teenager she shared part-board at a stable on a friend's quarter horse. She remembers another boarder, Ann Richmond, how her horse went colicky one spring and died, Ann at age fifty-one walking that horse for days and nights to turn the twisted gut right-side-up again.

"They call him Flipper, Flipper, faster than lightning." She and Louise used to know the words off by heart. "No one you see, is smarter than he."

The Jack Russell outside yips in his sleep.

"And we know Flipper, lives in a world full of wonder, flying there under . . ."

What kind of moment is this? she wonders, knowing it's mostly what she is now: alone, coarsened by time and love, regret brushing her face like a mane in the darkened paddock of night.

···

Back There

Janis peeled off her stretch-denim pants. Sassy, and smart – that's what Janis's mother had called them last fall when she placed the order by phone from the Sears catalogue, along with matching stretch-denim shorts, a hip-length jacket with a long pointy collar, even a stretch-denim poncho – though Janis had her doubts when, wearing the pants and jacket, she called for her best friend Monica on the first day of school and Monica's brother turned from the door to yell, Lumpy's here.

Now it was summer. For two days Janis and her mother had been sitting around the swimming pool at the airport Holiday Inn in Montreal studying the bathing suits and perfect bodies of Lufthansa stewardesses while Janis's father attended Expo ball games. To Janis's mother, originally from New Brunswick, this was the high life. She'd always wanted to travel.

On the third day Janis's mother insisted on a morning bus tour of downtown, with stops along St. Catherine for shopping. Too many choices, her mother kept saying, avidly circling the shoe departments: the pink vinyl or the white strappy sandals? She finally settled on the pale blue runners.

Worse, there were sheets and shams and tasselled things. Janis agreed: too many choices. She couldn't wait to get back to the pool.

In the hotel room Janis pulled on her terry-cloth bathing suit and ran outside. From above, the pool was a rectangle of light that levitated unsettlingly; she grasped the balcony railing for a second, woozy, sheer height lapping at her ankles.

Janis's mother joined her and together they lodged themselves in chairs on the pool deck. The women were out in full force: several at a patio table, ordering drinks from the waiter; two sunning themselves, artfully arranged elegant as dolls, swapping copies of *Der Spiegel* and *Elle*; and one in the shallow end of the pool, laughing, splashing water on her arms and tanned breasts, yipping sweetly at the cold.

Janis's mother surveyed the gingham bathing suits with white flounces, the plaid Sea Queen, the floral "Goddess" by Gottex (she had lingered over the same suit that morning at the Bay, she whispered proudly to Janis). Janis sensed her mother longed for clothes the way men longed for women – smoulderingly – in the old movies

Janis wasn't supposed to see but did, creeping down the stairs late at night to sit just outside the living-room doorway while inside her parents watched TV.

Janis herself longed for nail polish; it was the one reason she could give for wanting to grow up. Around her the women's extremities looked like fields of poppies waving slightly from the barest blush of a breeze.

After what seemed like hours, one of the women leaned forward in her chaise longue. She swung her legs around to one side and stood, towering blondely over Janis and her mother. The woman looked down and smiled at Janis. Janis's mother smiled back. Everyone, it seemed, was smiling, into the bright sunshine.

Janis, her mother said. It's time you and I had a little talk.

Janis soon stopped listening. Airplanes flew low in the sky. Her eyes hurt from looking at the pool. The highway beyond the chain fence rattled, something a baby might shake from time to time. She looked down at her body, laid out before her, plump, sunburned pink as a salmon at the Holiday Inn's lunchtime buffet table.

She looked about in desperation for something to throw over herself.

She longed for her poncho.

Fifteen years later Janis watched her mother in the swimming pool at the Lewiston, New York, motel, a woman terrified of the water though she had been taking a weekly Beginner Aquafit class for years. Through half-shut eyes Janis watched her mother in the shallow end. She held on to the side of the pool with both hands and bounced up and down, closing her eyes in concentration. Clearly, Janis thought, the classes had helped.

Boy, that feels good.

Water sprinkled Janis's face and arms, waking her. Don't stand so close, she said, clenching her teeth, a wad of molar and cuspid lodged deep in her mouth.

Janis, that sun's nice isn't it.

And she lay back in a chaise longue. Janis fell asleep again. She dreamed she was on a beach in Cuba, far away. She was happy. But then farmers burned the sugar cane and insects came. She woke up furious. She read Smollet; she read Austen. She was bored, tired. Her mother sat on the edge of her chaise longue, smoking, smoking.

Later that afternoon in the mall Janis wanted to die: to rise up out of the red three-button Henley her mother bought her at The Gap and leave it flapping in the dust, dust of dusts.

Janis, her mother said. Isn't this smart.

Janis stood by helplessly as her mother ordered up outfit after outfit, as if it were her job though she had stopped working years ago when she became pregnant with Janis. I'll try that in a medium, she demanded repeatedly, no matter how form-clinging, her round stomach bulging through elegant knitwear beneath a rayon vest printed with black and ivory diamonds.

Only two hundred and fifteen.

Janis stood so still she almost forgot to breathe. Snob! her mother cried after the shrinking saleshelp – busy, busy with other customers, with the cash register, busy with anything – who could hear, of course they could hear.

Up, Janis thought, the red shirt like earth dourly clinging to her hands, her feet. She knew if she looked down, she'd see her body white as salt beneath her.

In J.C. Penney they argued over intimate apparel. Janis's mother, who still used words such as *sizzle* and *pizzazz*, admired the denim-look Guess underwire bras with matching panties; Janis insisted on the black-and-magenta Gitano, trimmed with lace.

Wear it yourself, Janis finally said and stared at her mother, who grasped the Guess bra on its hanger.

I need more support, her mother said. She replaced the hanger on the rack. But I'd love to.

You're young, Janis's mother said over coffee, her Styrofoam cup kissed by lipstick. You can wear anything.

That night they went to hear Ella Fitzgerald in concert, her sequined voice like a sighting of silver through midnight trees, Janis thought, and shot through with shivery greens and golds. After the concert, Janis stood outside the pavilion, breathing slowly into a night flush with cicadas. A crescent moon was rising. She waited for her mother to reach the exit and locate her in the crowd. She didn't like being up so high, waiting like this; she wished her mother would hurry up so they could leave.

A dream, Janis.

Her mother was talking to her, though still a great distance below, trapped amid the leisurely exodus from rows P to T.

Janis, wasn't she just a dream?

Janis looked down at her mother, her moss-green linen suit a barest glimmer, like a memory. Janis knew years from now her mother would remember the event by what she'd been wearing. She saved everything, ardently: a pink cocktail dress, hot pants, *her* mother's fox-fur collar dark as loam in the cedar chest. That way, she once told Janis, she'd lose nothing. Besides, she liked to say, what goes round comes round. You might want them some day.

Janis stepped away, higher up the hill, then caught herself and stopped.

Janis?

Heads turned. Her mother was almost talking to herself.

Boy, she was saying. How old do you think she is? She must be getting on.

Janis's breath streamed into the cooling air. The flutter in her jeans caught her by surprise, wafting up to hold her, briefly, fiercely, by the throat. Tension, she thought. Butterflies. Though not quite the same as before. Now the jeans were looser, back to normal. Everything was back to normal, except for the occasional spotting; like the tension, a residue only. She'd almost forgotten.

Her mother caught up with her.

Janis, wasn't she just a dream, her mother was saying.

The next morning Janis wore the red shirt her mother bought her. They walked along a paved path on the American side of the Falls; Janis listened for its spin in her ears. She tried to keep her eye on her mother – always right up to the edge, leaning over the green railing. Janis! her mother called, and pointed.

We could try the Alpine ride.

Janis stopped and stared at her mother who stopped too, and looked out at the water and sky. Behind her mother's head Janis could see cables slung like tightropes from which, at regular intervals, tiny green cars dangled. From this distance they looked like toys. Janis thought she could see movement in one: two small figures at the top of the windy world, arms waving; they could almost be shouting, she thought, to make themselves heard over the wind, the wind itself pushing the shouting into their doll-like bodies, past dull wooden throats into bellies big as balloons. Janis half-expected them to float out the car window and rise, and never stop.

No way, Janis said to her mother. Not in a million years. Not on your life.

Janis's mother waited for Janis to start walking again.

Behind her left shoulder Janis heard her mother say, You're no fun.

Going home they crossed the border at the Rainbow Bridge. Around them cars hummed lazy as bees. Silver Accord. White Aerostar. Red LeBaron, top down. Janis and her mother in the Buick: almost through, after half an hour jammed into a line of cross-border shoppers. The Accord hovered briefly then floated away. Aerostar. LeBaron: nice-looking guy in Ray-Bans.

Janis. That line looks faster.

LeBaron removed his Ray-Bans, dreamily wagging his dimples at the customs officer who waved him on. Gone, Janis thought, slowly moving forward. Bastard. Beside her, her mother was scratching her hands, one at a time. She had never learned to drive, unlike Janis who, better late than never, now drove her father's car. Her mother twisted her wedding ring around on her finger. Janis, she said, strangely plaintive. Janis rolled down her window and pulled alongside the booth. Janis, she looks mean, her mother whispered, then leaned forward to smile toothily, like a dangerous animal, at the officer.

Toronto-Saint John, Janis and her mother said at the same time in reply to the officer's question. Integra-Sunbird-Civic behind them, a shining Supreme at the booth to the right: all that metal and exhaust stuck like gum to the asphalt, a congealed trail reaching back for miles into a promised land of discount malls, cheap Levi's, the candy-apple-reddest sunhats a heart could desire. Janis figured it didn't matter where you came from: no Canadian could resist.

The officer nodded.

As Janis pulled away from the booth her mother rubbed her hands together. Boy, that was close.

Why'd you buy so much? Janis snapped.

Her mother smiled serenely. It gives me a lift, she said.

Two hours later Janis drove her father's Buick over the Burlington Skyway. The wind nosed the car slightly to the left side of the lane; a moment later, to the right. Her neck hurt.

She glanced past her lane: sky blue as blown glass, the lake below industrial but wide all the way back to suburban Buffalo, to Tonawanda and Lackawanna. From high school history class she knew these were Iroquois names, that Toronto was Huron; to Janis they had always been tracts of land blank as textbooks. Only the fires were memorable: always a fire in Tonawanda, according to the Channel 7 *Eyewitness* newscast out of Buffalo every

Friday night before the late show when Janis was small. After the fire came either the Mummy, ancient and only vaguely Egyptian, or King Kong, locked gamely in the arms of an impassioned Godzilla. The station was also famous for displaying the sign Do You Know Where Your Children Are? during commercial breaks. Janis's mother always sat up with her and watched.

At the bridge's apex the pitch and shudder grew worse. Janis concentrated on the road so hard she thought her neck might break and her head roll off, glass-eyed and rigid as porcelain. She could see her mother breathe, and breathe and stop, each time holding her breath as if (it seemed to Janis) she thought she could will her daughter – poppet, small bleating thing – to safely traverse the Skyway despite the absolute lure and spin of the world.

Stop it.

Her mother jumped. What? she said. What did I do now?

Janis wanted to stretch, to ease her head to the left, to slowly count eight seconds before carefully turning her head to the right.

What.

The wide view stretching below, above; land seeping into a sky impossibly septic from industry, history, from everything that had ever happened. Janis wanted to point, chatter uncontrollably to her mother as they scudded behind a raft of eighteen-wheelers.

Though scared, she would have liked to.

Slowly taking her hands off the wheel.

They almost ran out of gas. Janis missed three exits; almost as bad, the gas station at the fourth was a self-serve.

Janis pulled into a gas bay and turned off the engine.

Do you know how to do this? Janis said. The butterflies in her stomach had turned to stone, weighing her down; something a bird might swallow to aid digestion. A lump: for four and a half months, that was how she had thought of it, despite her increasing belly. She thought she had rid herself of it.

Her mother sat motionless in the car. Do you know anything? Janis wanted to say but stopped herself in time. She got out of the car and saw, to her relief, the instructions on the pump.

She paid with her father's credit card. She also had his CAA membership card in her wallet; just in case, her father had said.

Did you have any trouble? her mother asked when Janis got back into the car.

What kind of trouble did you have in mind?

Half an hour later, just outside St. Catharines, Janis's mother wanted to stop. Back there, she said.

Fuck! Janis took both hands off the wheel.

Can you turn around?

Sure. I'll press the fly button.

Janis's mother was quiet for several minutes. She scratched her left hand.

Can I smoke in the car then?

Janis's heart lurched. Of course.

Her mother undid her seat belt. She leaned over and lifted her purse from the floor. I'll put the window down, she said.

You don't have to.

I better. Your father might find out.

Eight years after a triple bypass, Janis's mother still smoked, a fact of which Janis's father remained ignorant, despite the frequently used can of Lysol in the bathroom. Even at the time of the surgery, Janis's mother was un-repentant: she had been allergic to the anaesthetic and languished for ten days in intensive care, later becoming thin and jerky when Janis and her father went to visit in her semi-private room, a crazed puppet wildly halluci-nating; she kept pulling out her IV tubes before the nurses could catch her, hell-bent down the hallway for the smoking lounge.

Her mother never seemed to stop. Still not on solid foods, she called Janis at home one day and asked her to bring two orders of fish and chips – the Chinese ambas-sador was coming for dinner. And could Janis bring two Cokes? Three days later Janis perched on the ledge outside her mother's window, threatening to jump. Wearing, Janis's mother insisted, a baby bonnet. In the months that followed, her mother would be slumped for days and nights in a chair in the living room, hormones razing every micro-cell of her newly menopausal body, still achy and seemingly unrecoverable from the hole specialists had made in her chest.

Cigarette butts spilling from an ashtray – years later, driving the car, Janis could still hardly stand to think about it. In those days Janis's mother would occasionally fall asleep sitting up, cigarette in hand like a glowing watchful eye. Janis, spending half-nights taking in her jeans two inches at least along the inner seam, patching them, would stop on her way to the fridge for a Sprite, slide the cigarette from her mother's fingers, and put it out. Her mother hadn't dressed for days – weeks, even, it seemed to Janis, mutely slinking from kitchen to bathroom to bedroom.

Janis's father called from Edmonton. He called from Victoria. He seemed largely unencumbered, unlike Janis's mother grown heavy and loose in her skin as if enamoured of gravity, as if her body bitten back and bifurcated in a forcible entry of nature, rendering her a woman cruelly infarcted, her uterine heart inflected by gravity, with only gravity's nonsense sweet on her tongue. To Janis, her mother's odd clicks and moans, her grappling fingers a code Janis couldn't crack. Except for an unannounced fear, the look of her mother suddenly old and drooly, unsmiling into sleep. One cigarette. Two.

For weeks Janis came and went in that house – though not really, she never really went. When she lifted a Jonathan Livingstone Seagull T-shirt from Big Steel Man at Fairview Mall – she had skipped her double French class after lunch to do this – and wore it every day, empty (utterly empty) of intention, what could her mother do? alone in the living room, alone. Except to shout, You little bitch, you're not my daughter any more.

As if Janis's body were a steel door slamming shut in her mother's face.

What else could her mother do (her sweet seedlings lost to scorched earth, her babies finally gone)?

Threaten Janis with a broom at the bottom of the stairs until only Janis's opposite and equal threat caused her mother to stop and take to her bed, the house dingy as a cave and oddly carious, with Janis's mother gone so far inside Janis finally gave up calling, asking her mother if she wanted dinner: the frozen peas and carrots, the fried steaks and boiled potatoes Janis in her vague bewilderment made, silently moving about the small kitchen. (Her mother had not eaten for days – weeks, even, it seemed to Janis.)

In the end Janis left, taking a sleeping bag to various friends' houses, gone for weeks at a time. For years Janis and her mother were lost to each other in this way.

For the life of her Janis couldn't remember how she and her mother made up with each other. She only knew they must have, dimly, cautiously, because here they were now, together, in the car.

Janis's mother extracted a pack of Belmont Milds from her purse. She fumbled at the door, trying to open the car window. Janis, she said. Which button do I press?

Janis stopped at the next Tim Hortons. When they got back into the car Janis's mother rubbed her hands together vigorously.

Okay? she asked. Okie-doke?

We're like two children, Janis thought. Or one child-beast, twenty-four going on fifty going on ten, with two heads like the Push-Me-Pull-You in the Doctor Doolittle book her mother used to read when Janis was five.

Janis smiled. All right, she said. Okay. She put the key in the ignition.

Let's go! her mother said.

Years later Janis thinks she can't remember it all.

Up here on the third floor residents pad around in slippers and housecoats. Visitors bring fresh fruit and candied ginger, the damp smell of winter boots and coats.

Janis's mother sitting in a chair claps her hands in delight; and Saint John, New Brunswick – farmers in gumboots asking her to dance, her! in a pink satin sheath and white satin pumps, frosted pink and pearlized white plastic disks (by the dozen) on earrings that dangle, Chanel No. 5, everything she is able to remember – Saint John and its uncouth ignorant men fall away.

Janis marvels at how far her mother has come, from the Maritimes to Montreal to Toronto: a woman who weathered triple bypass at forty-two only to lose her mind at sixty. Janis and her father decided on the nursing home after Janis's mother broke her hip last fall, her alarmingly frequent wanderings halted only by a post-menopausal paucity of bone; her mother porous, filled with air and gone, Janis thinks, gone as far as sky. Janis can never catch her now.

Hello there. How's the hip?

Janis brings Cranberry Cove tea and sugarless Kisses, a can of Vernors, which she and her mother split.

There. Your hair looks better like that. Drink your tea I have to go soon. Put your sweater on, it's cold. Give me your mug. Please extinguish your last cigarette.

Mother, Janis thinks, I bear you no harm.

Janis takes her mother's mostly empty mug to the kitchenette down the hall, the fraught patter of other sons and daughters (all for the sake of the nurses, Janis thinks) provoking in her a chipping, a fury of white chinaware. She feels above it all; after all, her parents merely dim now, indifferent as Canadian Shield seen from the window seat of a plane. She thinks of bedrock sheeting entire provinces, nursing homes like fungal growths madly proliferating as North America ages.

She swishes hot water in the mug. Swish. Done. She puts it on the lined shelf. Waits, not really wanting to go back to her mother's room.

She should have had a plan. In and out, escaping with her life. And her mother's? Stuck, stuffed thoughtlessly and forever in a dress too young, too old, too flashy: Janis, I *need* something, I have nothing to wear, help me pick something – though her closet at home is crammed with herringbone, silk, pure new wool barely worn.

Too many choices.

Even so, Janis can finally see what's coming next, end of the road, obbligato heard on a car radio, one station seeping imperceptibly into the next as the same tune plays all the airwaves, her mother's slow alto push and scrawl counterpointing Janis's own ruthlessly spare and wordless manoeuvrings.

Janis. What should I wear?

As if a change of outfit could change a thing.

Janis knows she will go through her mother's accumulations, excavating the layers garment bag by garment bag, some thirty, almost forty, years old. *This* Janis will toss and *this* she'll keep and Goodwill will benefit mightily; at least there is comfort in that. Janis will stand before her mother's closet and what will she wear? (Now that her mother can't even dress herself, let alone Janis.

Now that Janis no longer plays dress-up.) The fifties are back in style. Or was that last year? The seventies are back; but Janis's mother was already old by then. In the high nineties Janis will stand in the body her mother gave her and think, *Two thousand*: in two thousand years my mother will be gone.

This is it, Janis thinks, walking back along the hallway to her mother's room: the wide view.

Janis comes by her prefigurations honestly, she knows, as she too swings low – this small inherited sadness in the dark months since November, the broody months in the steadily darkening years – all the way into her body, so like her mother's, an apple: round at the belly, genetically predisposed to heart attack and stroke and diabetes. Ways in which they let themselves, let everything, go. Janis and her mother still share a dangerously sweet tooth, the dark cravings tiding them through the raving months of winter, a series of days to be somehow gotten through despite a soughing from the belly, this ache, no baby.

No escaping. Only forgetting.

What she really misses are her mother's brave pinks and jaunty yellows. Sure signs of spring.

Janis, it's Janis, mother.

Janis?

Janis sits down on the edge of her mother's bed, then leans over to the night table. She picks up the phone and calls her father. Five rings, then the answering machine she bought him for Christmas comes on.

Soon there will be no one to love me, Janis thinks, long and hard, into the noonday sun; though she is often thankful for not having to share her thoughts with anyone. Outside it is almost April, warmish and watery-bright, though the sidewalks along Bathurst Street are still filthy with winter. She waits for the Lawrence Avenue bus as she waits for spring to arrive, a burst of colour – of fire-engine, Toronto Transit red – through the gusting greys of March.

Her morning classes are going well; she's a popular lecturer. Afternoons she works on her latest fatuous paper: "Patterns of Discourse in Trollope and Sterne." She works hard, though there are days when everything is a technical difficulty, days when she can't write a word, her putative skills notwithstanding. She waits for the MLA to publish her. She waits for tenure. She waits for her mother to die.

Tomorrow she will forget where she put her keys and worry for days. Slippage. The short or long skid marks off the road. Life, Janis thinks, at the Thrill-O-Rama: she has become the tightrope walker who briefly disengages to startle the audience in the back row, the special someone who might wave back (though not her mother – not any more).

She's suddenly acutely tired. She could almost, she thinks, fall asleep right here, here – buses and cars and trucks blasting the asphalt-grey earth, the begrimed March earth at the end of the world, blasting that world to cinders – and go no further. She could almost stop.

Janis's father's not home; she has let herself in with the spare key he still hides in the garage. There, at the back of her mother's closet, Janis finds it. The pink dress rustles against her shoulder. Chanel No. 5 warms her face, as if smoking from the floor beneath her feet – god, it all comes back: her mother's pandemonium body, the terraced grooves and slants, the great swoops and curls of hipbone to thighbone to anklebone. The hushabye hushabye baby.

Pink stuff falls into Janis's eyes.

Janis walk. Janis fall. Into her mother's waiting arms though a woman in heels could easily break a leg carrying a small and squalling child.

Earrings brush Janis's nose. She wants to open her mouth, taste them, until she remembers her mother's stinging slaps to prevent two a.m. trips to Emergency, X-rays, a child's heady foibles amidst the breakneck allure of the world.

Baby come to Mother walking falling.

Janis does, she remembers: her mother does her best, while Tonawanda flames forever behind them.

Here it is, Mother, Janis thinks, standing in front of the closet: the whole wide world.

Janis wonders if her mother would be very much surprised to know her only daughter drinks almost every day now; drives slowly, if at all. At thirty-eight Janis finds she is most like her grampie. He drank himself giddy once – up from New Brunswick for a visit shortly before he died – while the dark of a summer night grew all around him, swathed first his feet, then his legs, then his hands. He sang *Bye baby bunting* while Janis sat by the cedar hedge and waited for her mother and father to come home from a party, a swirl, a lapping, a slapdash of colour through the twilight, almost everything else reduced to light and dark, as in an old photo; her mother, Janis thinks, might have worn cerise, perhaps an ice-cream orange, organdy; though cool ivory would have been the perfect choice on such a hot night.

Janis knows she can't really remember. She'll have to take her mother's word for it.

arol's gone. He doesn't know it yet, but he will. Slowly, right leg dragging, he pushes the metal stand to the bathroom. The toilet flushes and he comes out, jerking across the floor. He parks the intravenous and grapples into bed. Plastic tubing extends from his arm to the bag hanging on the metal frame. I check his drip, quickly, before the nurse comes in: electrolytes in glucose solution, everything that's in him saline-serene. I examine the white switch on the tubing and find I can speed up the drip. I can slow it down.

He says, Carol! The word fuzzes slightly, his mouth twisting with great effort.

My stomach rises like heavy sweat. I'm on my knees on the bathroom floor when I extrude lunchtime soup and sandwiches, gesticulate wildly. What a bloody mess.

I get up. In the mirror I see Revlon Panne Rouge smeared to my chin, mascara like blackened starfish strewn – unfettered! – across my cheeks.

I search in my nice purse. There. I light up. I know what I know.

I take my plastic rainhat out of my purse and put it on. The streetcar comes. A woman scuttles past me. I ascend the steps, walk down the aisle and arrange myself, so, beside her. The poor creature's dreadful coat amply covers her seat and part of mine. I pretend not to notice, though I could tell her a thing or two. When I think of all the talking – on streetcars, in movies, their shirt buttons popping. TV, too, with its funny old girls, sphincters loose and flapping like tongues.

Now, Carol, I say to myself, what *could* you be thinking of? I open my mouth – god, I love my red Revlon mouth – and say, Nice day.

Home, I gently wipe the good soap to remove the dust; not too hard or the fluted lips of the seashell pattern dissolve. Periwinkle towels. Frosted containers of moisturizers, hair care products. I look in the mirror. A hot flush from my slight bosom to my cheeks surprises me. The Water Pik. Truly, all is vanity, I think, checking for

mildew behind the shower stall. I stop again and trace my
fingers over the burn. There, I think, there.

I pick up his Braun electric shaver and place it in the
wastebasket. There.

In the living room I take his favourite recordings of
Poulenc and Smetana from the teak bookcase. They make
a nice pile on the broadloom. Though it's four o'clock
and growing dark I don't turn on the lights. I sit in the
Brunschwig armchair I love so much. Light rain outside.
I open a new pack of cigarettes.

He collapsed yesterday at the top of the stairs, clutching
the tape recorder, saying, A pressure vessel, therefore
handle with care.

I think, *A pressure vessel?* I pause to put out my
cigarette, stalling. Twilight bites back each corner of the
room. I take a deep breath. To begin, I think. First things
first. A premise. And what should spring to mind but this:
my many years of service, pressure-tested.

I giggle, wondering what he would say to that, until I
remember I know the answer.

The frangible burst-disk assembly, he'd counter. He'd
thunder. Shut off the airflow.

A pressure vessel, steel or aluminum, contents compressed: handle with care, danger of – rust? I manage to
posit, voice quavery and small, cowering in the tasteful
expanse of the living room. Still, I press on. Flaky, I say,
recovering slightly, increasingly disputatious until I find

aluminum oxide, however, sticks – like my mind: I can barely muster a thought or two more, thinking: fringed curtains and, beyond, rain; the friable afternoon. Corrosion over and over.

In the basement I find the cardboard packing boxes from the TV, the VCR. I find milk cartons. I carry them upstairs. I take AutoCad, take Windows from his workstation shelves. Into the red Sealtest carton. In the kitchen I take five orange garbage bags. I walk up the stairs.

Second premise, a preliminary gas law: The pressure and the volume of a gas are inversely related; thus, the higher the pressure the lower the volume, and vice versa: Boyle's Law, applicable to everything that is under: the flatfish pressed madly to the bottom of the sea, the eel pout, the pelagic; even what crawled up out of a mucilaginous sludge how long ago, wingless, not fully formed; like my thoughts, once, high above the sea in Majorca, on vacation with my husband, as were she and her husband: all carapacious things, whether supple of skin or harsh of bone or that which is of the faint temerity of cartilage: all compressed under the pressure, the pounds per square inch, of atmospheres.

My husband, his brilliant mind. Carol, he'd said the first night in Majorca over dinner. This is my wife, Carol, faithful amanuensis.

Pleased to meet you both, I said. Nice weather we're having.

My husband. His brilliant mind, the weight of that knowledge, now mine, all that I've known for so long unstated: late one afternoon, watching her and my husband pick their way along the rocks, pressure increasing, volume decreasing. I could understand his attraction to her. She was quick and lively, she had a deftness about her eyes. They slid from object to object.

Waves crashed below. German tourists surmounted the hiking trails nearby. I counted three gannets above. Guano unspooled from them one by one. Behind me giant ferns slowly grew. I believe gingivitis to be the greatest evil facing man, her husband, sitting next to me, said.

My husband, his brilliant mind; that woman's glamorous mouth – teeth orchestrated by her husband, just so.

In the bedroom I sit on the bed, soothed by blond mahogany, the white eyelet spread with sham. The seven bright garbage bags shining beside me.

Pressure physics, I think, predictable: in addition, rust, corrosion, the frangible burst-disk, the friable stars at night swaying Boyle indeed all beasts in a vast Majorcan sea, a physics of air spaces and trapped colourless gases. My husband, his brilliant mind – also predictable, riven as an acolyte with the light of Boyle, loosed in front of his freshman classes (shining hopeful faces looking up), loosed and gleaming mechanical as a precision-engineered machine.

I stand and take a garbage bag, slippery as a conger. I go to the closet and open the door. Plaid slippers and matching dressing gown. Nitrous glisters, thin filmy bubbles of trace gases on my sloppy tongue.

Rain. Rain. In the living room again, I turn on the reading lamps. I get down on my hands and knees and take Bartok, Fauré, put them into the out pile. The Brunschwig, cream and rose, beckons. Instead I get up and go to the bookcase, crack the old philosopher Thales, my college-days Greek, his now vitrified though still-lustrous spine, his still-subtle aqueous humour. I am: crustal: dissolving to a strial, unannunciated vernacular, fleshy and notwithstanding.

My forehead swells and dampens. The reading lamps wick orange light onto the carpet. My shoes seem to stick like mud, subterranean creatures. I think, All the years typing, typing, as if holding my breath – I submit, a fierce embolus swelling: Boyle, aforementioned; furthermore, the whole chill world of pressure physics.

I throw Thales out as well.

In the hallway I take his hat. It sits on top of one of the orange garbage bags that I lug to the end of the drive-way. From the living-room window they seem to flicker in the rain.

•

The streetcar wails to a halt. Rain pisses down this morning. In that hospital bed the old man sleeps like God. God! asleep at the wheel. The very stars leak neutrons, the chlorine skies slice clouds and steam; and everything, damp streetcar teary babies, everything hisses even God, with God's green earth gone such a long time ago – and nothing to bring it back: not ten thousand lifetimes of wild orchids sobbing in air. He won't live long; he wanes, his palpable dust goes out of him; Death surely comes.

And I see a new heaven and a new earth: for the first heaven and the first earth are passed away; and there is no more sea.

Three streetcars follow behind. Thus are we four riding, crowded with mutterers, tense, reeking of morning rush hour.

I smoke in the hospital cafeteria. Years, I think. Years of not knowing my own alveoli. I pull the tin ashtray closer across the Formica table. Red lipstick-stained butts. Ash. Ash on my nice green pantsuit. Years of not knowing and now my thoughts run out of me.

Meanwhile his scrofulous cells tick and fester madly under glass in the basement laboratory, a chick-chick-chicking in the technological undergrowth. Not much time to lose. I sheathe myself in rich pleural, bronchioles glistening like a chandelier, lungs a room I enter with each breath I take young and radiant, every vascular impulse riding me in spills and twitches.

Behold, I think, behold I come quickly, until strangely livid I off-gas and rise.

The elevator chimes each floor as I float upward. Carol's gone; this time, as far as God: that's what I think.

Crush

Your mother told you to help the thalidomide boy. Coming from the girls' change room, bathing suit wrapped in your towel, you saw and immediately hated him, his flippers, his lousy boy's cowlick as he stood shyly by the pop machine at the Memorial swimming pool. You hated his shoes.

Always help those, your mother said loudly, less fortunate than yourself.

The can of Grape Crush slammed through the machine. You wondered how much worse it could get. You'd have to open the can for him. Maybe you'd have to hold the can to his pink dry lips. Wait to make sure the pop went down the right way. Wait for him to swallow. Tilt in some more.

You wondered how you could get out of it while the going was good. How to cut your losses.

Same as now, Saturday at Cherry Beach, the day feeling like one long week of Sundays and you blessed with catching the long tail end of this dusty afternoon. Stupid fuck, you think. He's maybe seven, eight. His friends fished him up out of the water. Two long breaths in, to start. Count five seconds. You think, Fucking kid.

You are cursed with a mind for statistics. Rescue breathing, cardiopulmonary resuscitation – you know the low success rates. Even so, you were glad to get paid time off from work to take the course.

Hey you, the instructor called out in front of the class when you administered an incorrect ratio of vertical compressions to ventilations to the plastic dummy. You just lost that sucker, he said.

That was – three years ago, five? You never went back for the recert.

Where, you think. Where the fuck's the lifeguard? Look up. There's no one there, no one but these wavering faces, looking at you. Someone says, Oh my god.

You, you say. You in the striped bathing suit, go for help.

You brush your cheek against the mouth. You have rechecked the airway for obstructions. You have repeated the head-tilt/chin-lift, exposing the thin white throat from which no reedy gargle issues. Carotid pulse – you can hardly believe you almost forgot to check for a pulse. You can hardly bear to think what might come next, you leaning over this limp broken machine, you sighting from the tip of a boy's lousy sternum with your fingers, the unbearable abrupt slam from the heel of your hand that will crush ribs and (you pray) not lungs and so begin the terrible pumping compressions. You – the one, the only – will not stop (not stop) until medical assistance arrives. A singular urgency announces itself, your hands now light as light and not metal urging metal.

Press your lips once more to this child's.

··

Scugog

Your husband turns the oldies station off and static whooshes like bats from the truck.

Why don't you listen to papa, he says and laughs.

Outside is goldenrod, white pine splendid at dawn, even a deer or two, you should be so lucky! but right now, a hundred thousand cars along Highway 57, their eleven p.m. lights smoking the oncoming lane.

Last night in the Cap' Martin motel he turned you over, blocking the St. Lawrence River from your view.

Baby girl, he said then groaned.

At breakfast early the next morning he smiled when you said, *Merci*, and, *l'omelette aux champignons*. Occasionally – over his scrambled eggs, sausage, juice – he held your hand. He hummed a tune. Your ring caught his eye. He twisted the band on your finger.

Merci.

The waitress smiled and refilled his cup, too. The much older American couple in the booth next to yours – unimpressed, pasty, impassive as angels – got up to leave.

Foreigners, you thought smugly.

Outside the river bluing to sky, where were you, Rivière-du-Loup? The drive home had been too far to make without stopping.

Can't get enough, he'd said last night, turning onto the exit ramp.

Almost home. Trees shift animal shapes in car headlights. Poplar, aspen, you think: a name for each. In front of you a red Corolla slaps the dust-choked road and ascends a hill, dips out of sight. To your right, Scugog, a muddy lake jammed with weeds and old tires, the ancient debris of ducks and gulls and red-winged blackbirds, shallow, not quite fourteen feet deep in the middle.

You skated there last winter. He held your hand as you stepped onto the ice. Then he grasped your arm and pushed you across. You thought of swollen carp moving sluggishly beneath you, slow burns.

Your arm throbbed for two days.

You'd met him at a Christmas office party. He was a supplier, holding court by the bulk photocopier. Amanda and Sue – single as you – eyed him hungrily, hot and driven. Hey hey good lookin'. Your pantyhose itched.

Around three o'clock he sauntered over.

After the bout of skating, during which despite his tender guidance you'd disgraced yourself by falling three times (still, how capably he'd put you on your feet again, brushed you off – how that felt), and over coffee thick with Haitian rum, he told you his first wife died of exposure, after the miscarriage and the separation. This was in the city, where lights and cold settle like dust on her grave, done – you'd thought in guilty satisfaction two weeks later, his left arm flung in sleep across your right thigh, his quartz heater burning steadfastly through the drafty Port Perry night – over with, *finito*.

No compensation for the dead.

No pity, alimony, late-night calls, and the glass of water beside the phone beading with sweat.

A bad stretch of road. He follows closely behind the Corolla, driven by a woman, you can tell by the hair, the small shape of the head, fox-like. In the lights from passing cars trees shift hands, a finger, necklace, on her throat. The Corolla wanders into the now-empty oncoming lane then pulls back. He gears down to third and speeds up. Hits the high beams.

You imagine her hair long unlike yours, short wispy blonde, hers the dark plush of a mink, weasel, her tiny polished teeth growing like fear in her mouth.

Don't ever leave me, he said last night in the motel.

It had all happened so fast: the courtship, marriage, the honeymoon. At this age a good man is hard to find, so you'd jumped. He made you feel so good, like honey, sweet lambs gambolling, and the way he expertly aimed your hips.

Last night you'd purred like a – kitten? You did: against his shoulder. He made you feel so young.

He eases up on the gas. Leans back, right arm resting over the top of your seat. His hand makes a hillock of your neck.

He wants to get you a car phone. These days you never know.

Now you imagine a car stopped by a ditch seconds before abandonment, a young woman slipping into the night, into the weed-choked lake where police dragged for three days last spring.

Was it Cross? The Cross girl. They never found the body. It was all over the papers.

●

And the others, the ones from Blackstock, from Oshawa.

Havelock, too.

The red Corolla turns right at Enniskillen. You're strangely relieved.

You're so quiet, he says. What are you thinking?

You turn your precious face to him and smile cool delectable thoughts. You ride like this, all the way home: he arouses you. He didn't his first wife, you're sure of that.

Your name is Sharon. You say this softly, once or twice, to yourself. *Sharon Rose.*

His name too, now yours. *McNeil.*

Still later that night, the lake – a pit of longing – will open to croak up its dead like a bullfrog, you think upon awakening, though you've never seen one, you who have come from the city.

He'll climb back into the creaky bed. You'll wonder where he's been.

Hiya sleepy head, he'll whisper. Hey there, sleepy thing.

···

Boy

I saw an ocelot, bag of bones with lime-Jell-O eyes. A nest of mud snakes, glazed in the heat like ham. The peccary is indigenous to North and South America. It has sharp tusks, small erect ears, and a short tail. The Virginia opossum is variable, but prefers woodlands. The young attach firmly to a teat and remain there for fifty-five to seventy days.

Did you know each toe of an even-toed ungulate ends in a hoof?

An example is an old world swine.

Texas sliders: most of central Texas and Pecos River. Suwannee cooters: a turtle of the clear spring runs; also occurs in the turtle-grass flats off mouths of streams.

Mudpuppies waving crimson gills. Skin not toxic like many other amphibians.

A bowl of meat dipped in raw egg, smell rising like a man's throat.

Hold your nose, Jamie, my mother said.

A woman squealed.

At the gorilla enclosure two boys tossed sticks. My mother watched from a bench above the dirt path. Smart, she said loudly. The biggest boy screwed up his face at the male gorilla, who mimicked him, then spat green stuff into a black palm and showed it to the crowd. I observed closely the ears and snout, as if cutting a picture from a *National Geographic* my aunt used to send from Florida, curls of paper like toenail clippings on the floor. Sometimes I glued pebbles shaped like molars, tufts of hair from the neighbour's dog to the scrapbook page.

The boys huddled close to the Plexiglas. Judging by height, I bumped the youngest. His face folded. Adam, do a payback, the older one said. Trash him. My mother said, Jamie. She sipped her soda, every now and then holding the cup to her wide sweating face, white as the peeled potatoes she cut and french-fried six days a week in the back of our truck in Picton. With her free hand she lifted her long thick hair, tangling wet off the back of her muscled neck, and shook it. The boys shuffled off, turning every half-minute or so to look at me. I eased toward them through the Sunday crowd, endless baby strollers, cotton candy, my strawberry Yoo-hoo drink – from my decreasing Florida supply – warm from the sun.

Adam, whispered the bigger boy. He shook a box of Chiclets. A-dam.

II

A hundred garter snakes. A hundred-hundred milk snakes.

This was in Fort White.

The first one I saw – rubbery, dry – was wrapped around a leg of the table off which we ate. The second, third, and fourth to seventh scraped furiously under the door to the small storage space off the trailer bathroom, where I'd left them, popping against the sides of a green garbage bag. I'd collected them at lunchtime for my science project, two days' overdue.

I opened the storage space door. The bag was broken. Snakes flailed the air.

Honestly, my mother said. She stood in the doorway above me, half-blocking the light. She came one step down the stairs. Snakes parted from her feet. Holy jumpin'. Her eyes shone in the semi-dark. She put her hands on her broad hips.

Let's get these out. Pronto.

She turned and stepped back into the hall. Snakes flipped after her up the last step.

Outside the trailer the tall grass lolled. She knelt beside me, right knee creased with scars from an operation. Her square hands, also scarred, leaked grease from the truck's deep fryers onto a brown paper bag that she opened carefully. Seven snakes wrinkled across the narrow drive.

She said, So much for homework.

At school I was average and slipping, dull as rain, what I could figure of meridians, the square of the hypotenuse filling me like an old tin can. At night I slept rust: sea salt, inland springs, Crystal River, the manatees. Spanish moss. Sky red as blood-shame in my ears when Jan-Elizabeth kissed me Wednesday morning at recess, and her girlfriends laughed loud as cicadas.

This was in Madison.

In Perry I play burnball every day after supper, making do with Mike Hires, a retard from Special Ed. class. Slap-slap down the road, smoking ball against glove faster-fast through the long twilight, everything flattened to two boys one creature purely boy, and a sound like spitting.

There are days and days of this.

And fire when I torched the fort with kerosene stolen from the neighbour's shed. Inside the plywood walls one of the boys said, Steve and Jerry. Another one said, No, Ken. I swear it was Ken.

They were older than me. The fort was their meeting place, and I followed them there several times a week for a month until they saw me slipping after them among the trees.

War. My face had ached for days. Now, crawling belly down beneath the skewed hole they called a window, splashing the walls from a tin can, I stopped to wipe sweat from my eyes, crying oil.

Maybe Steve and Ken.

No way. Was not.

More fuel. A dribble leaked from my nose. Then smoke and flame, a million boy-voices lifting to oaks' old arms high above my escape route.

I made myself scarce for weeks.

Gradually I began to come around again, four o'clock on the outskirts of school, fast squeezes of gravel aching from my bike's tires, girls whose names I never learned twisting in fear when I lunged for their breasts.

If you live near a spring or swamp, you too can collect specimens. Look for mole skinks (family Scincidae) in

areas of sandy well-drained soil. The positions of the lon-
gitudinal stripes are important. Count downward from
the midline of the back. As in: "stripe on 5th row."

Rule out whiptail lizards by checking back and belly
scales.

Hellbenders thick as cushions in specimen jars, tasselled gills waving red.

Palmetto bugs larger by night when I thought I'd
turned the light on in the kitchenette and squashed one,
then woke suddenly, wet in the bed.

The terrible scent of almonds.

Boy. Pecker like a roach, my mother said.

That was in Branford.

One fall afternoon I heard the truck pull into the drive
earlier than usual, the bump and bang of pails of grease
she'd change only once a week. What do *they* know, she'd
say of her customers, mostly people just passing through
who she'd never see again. Let them complain.

I knew she hated being questioned. I'm fit, she'd say
after the few parent-teacher interviews she attended at
my schools. After the fort burned she'd said, Just let
them try.

I hadn't been to this new school once this fall, but I
didn't think she knew. When she opened the front door
and stepped inside I had an excuse ready. But she didn't
seem to notice me as I leaned against the kitchenette

counter. She put her bag on the sofa and lifted her left hand to the side of her face, cradling it. She stumped slowly around the room, picking up objects – an old perfume bottle her last boyfriend scrounged diving on the bottom of the river, a giant pine cone her sister bought years ago at a gift shop in California – with her right hand as if weighing all that was past and would never come back, figuring what she could add in or take out according to whatever sense she could make of things to come.

Finally she said, And that's the name of that tune. She put down a white plaster angel she'd been considering.

Jamie.

She came over and took my arms, held them out to her. Then she pinned me, quickly, to the stove, its chipped enamel like teeth marks.

You little bastard.

She let my arms drop. You fucked up, she said. We're out of here. We're goners.

We spent that night at my aunt's in Lake City. Her house was unfamiliar to me, slipcovers on the sofa and soft chairs, and my own room to sleep in.

My aunt had never married – unlike my mother, who'd left my father when I was two, divorced him when I was five – and lived alone in a small bungalow bought with her portion of their mother's inheritance. The *larger* portion, my mother called it: my aunt had looked after

the old woman in sickness, who never forgave my mother
for leaving. For years the two sisters hardly spoke. My
aunt was nuttier than a fruitcake, my mother said – her
sister periodically checking into a private clinic in Tampa
– just like their mother. And as loaded. She was younger
than my mother, though they looked alike, my aunt
being slightly softer, puffed up and melting where her
makeup ran.

I woke the next morning to my aunt opening the
bedroom door. Rise and shine.

It was late, ten o'clock at least. I said, Where is she?

Come on, lazy bones, let's get cracking.

She walked all the way into the room. I pulled up the
covers. Where did she go?

She snapped back the navy blue curtains and opened
the screen window.

Your *mother*, she said. Your *mother*.

At Wal-Mart my aunt buys extra packages of t.p.

In case we run out.

She laughs giddily, winks then rolls the cart to the
ladies' undergarment aisle, her ankles spongy beneath
green pants.

Orange blouse.

We go to the Waffle House for lunch, homefries scattered smothered covered. Chunked? the waitress says.

Not chunked. My aunt says, Are you sure? and the waitress winks.

I am sure.

The drive home on roads shiny as sheet metal, leftover steak leaking through the doggy bag onto my lap. A sudden rainstorm bends branches over the road. Just as suddenly, the storm's over.

Well, hello sunshine.

A white chair.

Jamie, do you like peas?

That night there was a map of the universe on the ceiling of the room I was now supposed to call mine, star light star bright first star I see tonight bright as the Happy Face Nite-Lite my aunt bought, oblivious to my age. My mother was still gone. Cassiopeia. Polaris. My aunt's light went out down the hall. The house smelled of freshener and fish cakes.

I got out of bed and flicked on my light. After a moment I turned it off and got back into bed. Ursa Minor, Arcturus, small points of yellowish-green, sparked above my head and somewhere outside, firestorms, the collapse of suns and cold distance seeping across the fields of night. The Great Horse Nebula on a hot tear through the fissure cracks and bedding planes of the covering sky. The Happy Face grinning like mad.

Sirius-Arcturus, bright and early, rise and shine. My aunt took the wet bedsheets from my hands.

Uh oh, Geronimo.

Bitch.

My aunt turned to me and said, Go upstairs. This was my fourth day alone in the house with her. I had just finished my third Pop-Tart, and now my mother stood on the front steps to the house, impressively kicking the door.

Ellen, please, my aunt said.

My mother thumped the door with her fists. Joy. Give him back, Joy.

My aunt began to cry, slowly shrugging her shoulders. She leaned against the wall and held her stomach as if in her softness something hard and precious might slip to the floor and shatter.

Ellen, don't make me. He's mine. Not yours.

That night my mother and I rode in the truck past Luraville, the road sourly rolling as I knew she'd rolled from Texas once, to Florida's gulf side, slicks moving in like sadness from Corpus Christi, the Padre Islands of her childhood. It was a clear night, and the town lights skipped like stones in the truck's rear-view mirror. She turned onto the dirt road to Telford Spring.

She fucked us. I tried to fix things but she fucked us over.

I didn't say anything. The truck bumped along until we reached the clearing. She stopped and said, Here we are.

Thin clouds coiled in the sky. Something hissed at the night then was silent. Through the windshield the water seemed slippery as vinyl. At first only the occasional splish-splash or a low soft guttering heard through the open window gave depth to the tannic river. Neither of us said a word, as if we were waiting for something too important to miss and we wanted to be ready for it.

I could tell from her sharp breathing that she was still fuming. I twisted my back to the door on my side and stretched out anyway, feet in her lap. She snagged my ankles in her hands, and held on tight. The night wore on, the stars above and below the billion wink-sinkings of patio lights. Gradually I forgot right side up and upside down. Fog slid in. I slept.

The next morning we were almost to Valdosta when, as if she still clutched my ankles, I leaned out the truck window, sick onto the I-75 shoulder.

Count the wrinklies, she said each time we passed an
RV of old people heading south from Canada. Her half-
brother lived there.

We passed our fifth Airstream. How many was that? she
said. Sixteen? I think that was sixteen.

My small thoughts slipped like pennies all the way to the
Ontario border, to Scarborough, to Picton – like the
allowances my aunt sent, whatever small change my
mother passed on to me and I spent on black balls,
the layers sucked past orange, robin's-egg blue to grey the
colour of Lake Ontario boiling from the Bay of Quinte to
Point Traverse where rum-runners once ran and the wet
bones of old sailing ships – the *Annie Falconer*, the *Olive
Branch*, *City of Sheboygan* – lie in cold silt off False Duck
and Amherst Island. Where the money from my aunt
stopped coming as winter steam lifted in sheets off the
lake warmer than forty-below air.

When the snow turned to rain then to fever and fog I
heard a voice tumbling like rags inside a washer saying,
Catch me if you can, dissolving in acid, stretched to a
shape I couldn't recognize, hung to dry on the crackle-
breath of jaws.

Anhinga, snake-bird.

Old copies of *Gator* USA, hoarded for centuries.

My mother who runs the chip wagon. She is old and I must do my best to love her, greasy, a mottled anger cooking her bones – in a cold cold land and I do not belong.

My mother's touch soft as the Velveeta I began to crave in spring. A sure sign, she said, I was getting better.

In summer, leopard frogs sundering the lighthouse road as I walked, shush-shushing into the long grass, amphibian hearts turning blue in their cold chests. A hundred-hundred hundred snakes. And I a follower of science.

III

CROCODILIANS. American alligator (*Alligator mississippiensis*). Black with yellowish lines. Head smooth in front of eyes.

Curved bony ridge - - - - ➤
Fourth tooth - - - - - - ➤

You may observe eyes, snouts protruding from water surface of holes along waterways of the south.

All sizes bask.

My mother fanned herself with a zoo guide. Her empty soda container sat at her feet. She smiled at a young woman in a yellow sunsuit who bent over a small girl and roughly tucked her shirt into her pants. In the exposed part of the woman's breasts tiny blue veins jumped like electrical currents. Before straightening she jerked the girl's pants up. The child rose two inches off the ground.

I pulled a peanut from my pocket, shucked it one-handed and flicked the shell. It bounced at Adam's feet. My mother wasn't looking. Adam, I called softly. His friend's Chiclets whispered in their box.

Quit following that boy around – if he jumped off a bridge you'd go too.

Adam, eyes open wide. Pale colouration, short red hair. Approx. four feet, two inches.

I took a swig of my drink.

The spectacled caiman is small and has a bony ridge between the eyes. Problems of identification occur only in Florida. In the American alligator the snout is broad and rounded in front.

A woman sat next to my mother on the bench. Boys, the woman said. My mother said, I know what you mean. You can say that again. She clicked open her purse. She said, Jamie.

I put my Yoo-hoo on the concrete ledge above the enclosure. CAUTION. DO NOT LEAN. Nothing in the pool below me moved. The surface was green, thick as brine from a pickle jar.

The fourth tooth, while enlarged, fits into a pit in the upper jaw and is not exposed at the side when jaws are closed, as in the American crocodile.

More soda, my mother called. She pulled a five from her purse.

Voice. Adult male: throaty, bellowing roar. Adult female: grunts like a pig when calling to her young, which she may protect from predators. Young: high-pitched, moaning grunt – like saying *umph-umph-umph*.

I leaned over the railing, looking in. A musky unpleasant odour.

Alligators of all sizes hiss.

Adam watched as his friend edged closer to the railing beside me. Chickenshit. Buck-buck-buck buck. The Dickey Dee wagon was coming through. When I looked again not even my mother was there.

IV

I'm freckled. Jeans rolled up, my high-tops on. It's 1993.
BOY EATEN BY GATOR. Another headline might read, BOY
KILLED AT ZOO. But I'm down here, I'm down here still.
(Turn the page. See?) Keeper pokes at me and the crowd
thrills to my sluggish moves. At night his pole glows
verdigris, the lights of my pool like stars dragged down
from the sky to where they hiss and gurgle.

Here's another.

A boy peers over the low railing. Cowlick. Peanut fists.
Red-stained mouth, Tahiti Treat. He leans closer. There's
a moment when the crowd looks away.

Yoo-hoo, I call.

Baby Jesus and the Intruder

Sometimes there's so much dirt. Baby tells Lee there's so much dirt he can't get himself clean. But that's not here and he tells Lee that, too. Not here in Karla's nice house – skylights, white bookcases, full reno in bad neighbourhood – where all that's dirty are his hands from wrapping newspaper all day long. Counting, tying, he and Lee listening to the radio, ink all the hell over them. Papers from Italia, *la belle* France, lots of Commie papers. All these beautiful human communities in the cracks and pores of his hands, and he's holding them, licking the ink sometimes when he eats a sandwich from Karla's fridge and forgets to wash.

Sometimes he dreams in languages he can't understand. He's talking sweet and pure, and everybody in the dream's nodding and smiling, perfectly happy. When he wakes he doesn't know what he was saying, why everyone was smiling so hard. What all those words were.

That's something he doesn't tell Lee.

He moved his stuff last night, right after he'd finished his gig, telling Anita, This is one shit-joint. Then he added, I don't care where you were.

She flicked her bangs out of her eyes and it was too much – more than the nights she never came home, more than his dates playing at Lee's Palace that she never seemed to make – an act not to be borne.

See this guy here? he screamed, pointing at his bare scrappy chest.

Anita blinked as if breaching some strobe-lit dance floor way past closing time, pale princess he could never get out of bed before noon though once up she *was* a sexual athlete: once before her first smoke, then again after coffee, thin arms waving slowly above her head, eyes opening and closing as if in time to last-night's music, lost to it.

Who do you see? he screamed though he knew when she was like this he could never get through to her, this strange call – Whoo? – twisting his voice half-human, a dry adenoidal screech rising octave upon octave in some corner away from the lights, this place he feared, where the touch of his hands could never save her, she was a case and he was sorry, sorry he'd never been able to make her come twice.

Whoo-whoo, he called as she crawled under the kitchen table and put her fingers in her ears, yellow hair masking her face. She rocked back and forth, knees drawn to her chin, bare slim feet crossed elegantly at the ankles.

He stopped only when he realized he himself didn't know the answer.

Late last night on the phone Lee said, Space is real.

Too real, he told her.

This morning Lee picks him up at Poppy's tiny restaurant in front of the Oak Leaf Steam Baths. It's early, eleven, maybe eleven-thirty. He finishes his eggs and Poppy says, Pay me later, Baby. On the way out, past toys and knick-knacks, truly an amazing collection, neon-pink squirt guns lying on the counter, little chickens and houses and sheep from Red Rose tea boxes arranged in tableaux, he remembers to introduce Lee to Poppy.

They look at each other and nod slightly in that chill way women have sometimes: all these bitch queens trying to score a place higher on the food chain.

Lee knows the game, only a year ago escaping first Hamilton then Women's Studies at York University (he'd been worried, they'd known each other since junior high school and that made her his oldest friend alive) to luck into a condo on King Street with her new butch mama.

Now Lee eats sushi instead of Miss Vickie's potato chips for dinner, drinks sake instead of beer though not too much or the boss-woman's out.

Today Lee's got her new honey's nice new car.

Baby misses Lee's junker, though, a '69 Tempest the police finally towed away for good last month, parking tickets like dead leaves jammed under the right and only windshield wiper. When it rained Lee would lean way over to the passenger side, steering precariously through the dark treacherous streets while visions of hydro-planing danced in their heads.

As Lee swings her girlfriend's car left onto Bathurst Street nostalgia suckers him big time, in the stomach, diesel fumes from passing trucks swooping in like stealth bombers. He sinks lower in the bucket seat, checks to make sure he's still alive.

Feet, he cries out, are you with me? though when he checks leg bone to knee bone everything seems okay.

Lee makes a right turn.

Where you going to go, feet? Your old walking shoes done gone.

Lee laughs, changes lanes. He punches it out now, Baby baby baby – Lee hammering the car in and out of traffic on Dundas Street, slugging it back and forth from one side of the streetcar tracks to the other – Baby, where you got to go?

He supposes he's still here, in one piece, wailing knee to hip to – but the smooth ride of this pricey car, his torn jeans against its tan leather interior, take the jag right out of him.

He sinks even lower in the seat. He sees Lee check the rear-view mirror then glance at him, wanting more. She can forget it. Today he's cooked, head and hands and: bone-sucking creeper, he thinks, his tendrilled heart withering, wasted.

The first thing he does when they get to work at Karla's is: he terminates an earwig for Lee.

Run, you little bastard. Then bam with his thumb on the dining-room table.

Squashed that sucker flat, Lee says, impressed.

Next he shuts down the house alarm, installed after the third break-in, so he and Lee can open the sliding door off the sunroom in the back and unload the van, then load it up again with newspapers for tomorrow's run.

He turns the radio on.

Then he heads for the kitchen.

Karla has beautiful plates. They're light blue, hand-thrown in Quebec City. He pours coffee into a matching cup and puts it on the faux granite counter. The old woman who looks after Karla's baby and who's been here since eight o' clock comes into the kitchen, sees him, quickly leaves.

He helped Karla paint this room (plum-my) when he first came back from tour in England. Anita wasn't speaking to him though he'd catch sight of her at the Squeeze Club and know she'd seen him: she'd flip her hair over her shoulder and laugh loud at some guy's remark.

His heart would unzip. Thoughts of her hard little mouth would hurtle out and hang halfway to the floor, trolling indecently. He'd feel exposed, have to haul ass out of there before he broke every obscenity law in the book and got busted for love, before she laughed one more time at beauty boy's joke, before he dragged her outside to pound her cunting head into the sidewalk.

He picks up his coffee and wipes the counter with a dishcloth from the sink. After the first couple of weeks like this Karla called one day from the CIDA office where she organized special relief projects for developing nations. He'd met her a year earlier, when he'd performed at a fundraiser for the agency. She'd taken an interest, come out to hear him at other dates. Introduced him to friends. Invited him to dinner.

I think you need a little responsibility, she'd said that day on the phone. She was right. For those first few months, he'd wake on a futon in Karla's sunroom not knowing if he was coming or going, Anita still a great yowl tearing his chest from the night before, then he'd get up to paint and wallpaper and take the garbage out and change the cat litter. Once he tried to fix the eaves-troughing that was coming down in places until Karla found out he was afraid of heights and hired an old-guy handyman who hacked streamers of green spit into the yard all day as if planting vines.

He gave up smoking. He began to eat better: tofu shit and broccoli and brown rice. He was, he began to realize, one of Karla's special pets, a project, and that after all that time on tour in England, coming back burned out at twenty-three years of age, he was neither coming nor going but was in fact staying put for a while.

Going nowhere.

Couldn't have been a better place for it. People would drop by all the time, contacts, maybe, even the strippers-turned-performance-artists that Karla would help with arts grants forms. He'd play the barker in everyone's booth, riffs like sparks flying off bumper cars at a midnight midway as he *did* them and they loved it, showing them whispers of dreams like prizes showering the night, *Try your luck with me*, and he'd feel good, at home in his skin, as if anything he wanted could happen.

Like, he'd say, listen to this, Liza talks! And Karla's friend Liza – a newly divorced sound editor and really not bad-looking – would lift her wineglass high as if toasting him.

Listen, he'd say. You got a new coat, black, but I can see it crushes you, this it's-all-over coat. You've left a soufflé full of tears rising in the kitchen, your heart like corn husks lying in the sink. Liza, where you've been gone so long? and his voice would drop a trombone moan.

They ate him up.

When Karla's friends christened him Baby Jesus Jackson – hours spent drinking good red wine from nice wineglasses, listening to Smithsonian blues collections, borrowed ache steeping their bones – it was a joke, educated, hip.

But it worked. Lee tells him she's seen his tape, *Baby Jesus Here/Now*, at This Ain't the Rosedale Library when she delivers their newspapers.

One of the guys who works there's even heard it.

He finishes his coffee. Lee's talking on the phone to her girlfriend. He takes the empty cup to the kitchen and rinses it. When he returns Lee's still on the phone, cord wrapped around one finger, head cocked to one side. Yeah, she says softly. Oh yeah. He slips a set of keys off a hook on the wall, slides open the sunroom door, and steps out. Factory and waterfront smells – Lever Brothers Detergent, Redpath Sugar – nestle in the thickening midday air.

Lee, he yells, not even turning around. Get your ass out here and help me.

Somewhere in the great beyond pigeons rumble.

Lee. Come on come on.

A starling scrapes distractedly in the stone bird bath. For a few seconds the sun burns through the haze, then the sky yellows again. He unlocks and lifts the van's back door. About thirty bundles of newspapers and magazines wedged inside. Lee. For god's sake. Help me. Please.

Counting. Tying. Tearing title and date strips off the returns.

Karla says for him to count and Lee to tie because Lee, who's left university to attend trade school in the fall, doesn't need to hone what Karla calls her numeracy skills, as he does to fulfill the conditions of the Ontario Futures program that actually pays him.

He's got to hand it to Karla. When she got the idea to become an alternative newspaper distributor (herself remaining full-time with CIDA), starting the company with Ontario small-business loans, hiring employees through Futures, it seemed perfect for both of them: skills-development and stability for him; political cachet, cheap, for her. Because of her contacts, his form went through quickly: the case worker owed Karla, who'd once hired a paranoid schizophrenic the worker had referred. He hadn't worked out – he claimed Bruce Springsteen ripped him off for several hits he'd written during the eighties (who knew if it was true), and it gnawed at him continually – but a favour's a favour any way you slice it.

Still: all these returns. Sometimes they get to Baby. Karla's mission – read, read, and the word my brethren is: Feminism, Marxism-Leninism, (I say) Eco-war (and do some) Deconstructionism, for you *are* the disenfranchised, monopolized disembodied-disembowelled multitudes and you are standing at my door and *I* shall feed you my babes in the woods for you have wandered far – all that smack-back in her puss.

As for himself, he picks his cheque up once every two weeks, at the Futures office on Queen Street. Two months after starting work he got back with Anita – to Karla's dismay – and together they moved into a bachelor on Dunn Avenue. Paydays he'd splurge, buy steak and shrimp, beer, a carton of Lucky Strikes for his girl whose tip-money from dancing paid the rent and whatever niceties she began to like too much and nothing he could do about it – him sucking the public tit, unable to support her himself, this fact a constant banging on his brain.

Ah, Futures.

He remembers the interview to assess his suitability for the program. In a church basement where sun swung through a low window in trapezes of dust.

Ladies and gentlemen, sign here please.

Karla and the case worker stared at him expectantly. Baby picked up the pen and his heart quailed.

Saul Appelbaum.

Ah, Karla said. Deal made in heaven.

Around one o'clock he and Lee get good and cracking. They switch jobs because he doesn't add and subtract so well and Lee doesn't like to cut herself on the twine, never mind the fresh scrapes on her hands and arms turning to scars daily before his eyes: her new honey not so nice sometimes but, he figures, whatever blows your skirt up, that's love for you.

He just can't imagine doing it himself. Not even mild slapping. He liked to think that with Anita it was different, that it was love-making, though of course Anita called it fucking. That's what she'd said the first time they met, at a party. She'd walked in on him in the bathroom and said, Wanna fuck? She hadn't looked him in the eye. Later, when they were living together (it took about a week for her to leave the old boyfriend's place and move in with him) he'd say, I want to make love to you, and her eyes would narrow.

She rarely looked the same way twice. He could never anticipate her moods, she was crazy, fucking crazy – god, within two weeks of living together she had him ripping off tampons for her from the Becker's down the street, Anita with a pretty summer dress on and no money, *I've got my period* she announces and people are looking, of course no underwear on either so he'd had no choice, that was love for you, just made you crazy all the time.

But when he wanted to make love he could expect a look pure as hate to lift like a veil of smoke from the mask of her face. She'd put her cigarette out and lie on the bed, staring at the ceiling as if to say, Fuck me then, asshole.

Come to think of it, he *could* have slapped her sometimes.

He slits lengths of twine like there's no tomorrow, slings bales of paper out the back door. Lee's got the calculator out.

Slam bam thank you ma'am. Faster this way.

The radio's on loud. The old piece who looks after Karla's baby creaked upstairs a long time ago. Shouting over the music Baby regales Lee with the saga of his latest career dilemma: Hazel – that Hazel, the very one – wants Baby to tour Kentucky with him just like they toured England together.

Lee says, Cool.

But, Baby points out, right now he couldn't take it, Hazel some kind of delta-punk crazy like Baby'd never heard before: music in pure guitar slashes like a cat gutted and strung up by jerks on the baseball diamond on the way home from school, blood on fur ten feet high on the fence – little kid and the first time he knows this kind of thing happens and now the whole world's different, going to go home and open that front door and where'll Mom be now?

Hazel knows ain't no place like home.

Not for a hard-driving man called away by each false delight calling itself the answer. One day you wake, put on your walking shoes and get good and gone, legs waltzing one way, fingers snapping another. There is another calling as each crackling rib renders a love a loss. Each ache and fat fuck and extravagant tender time calling down the grime of the world in great whacks of bone-handle spinning through chunks of chips and spit and newspaper, filling your spaces until baby you be gone so long with no place to call your own.

Hazel. He showed Baby some places, a thousand plates of eggs and chips. In England audiences had been small.

That's all everything is: just places.

At two o'clock Baby switches the radio station over to Buffalo.

As usual, Karla calls at two-thirty to remind them to turn the house alarm back on after they've finished loading the van.

Hey, pretty mama, Lee says into the phone. Like, no problemo, eh?

While Karla talks Lee – also one of Karla's projects (*employ a lesbian today*) though Karla deeply resents not being consulted on Lee's change of status from marginalized gender-bender (*resist!*) to passive other in a bad-consciousness relationship (*quel embarrasse-ment!*) – rolls her eyes, brandishes her tongue in the air.

Yo! Baby says brightly to the plants he's supposed to water Mondays and Thursdays. Takes a lickin' and keeps on tickin'.

At three o'clock he tunes in to CKLN-FM for the weekly club listings. They get his date right at Clinton's. A minute later Lee's screaming, *I'm* a Quaker S/M lesbian, slighted at something the announcer said.

Her blue eyes widen as they did in junior high once, some asshole knocking her halfway down the stairs for being out.

Like, you know, she says to Baby. Fuck, he says, and, For sure – because he really does know.

She turns surly, half hellhound snarling, Babylon, before exiling herself to the basement.

The day blows hot, the day blows cold.

Maybe he'll call Cheaters. See if Anita showed up for work. Maybe her face isn't messed up too bad.

When he first met her she worked at Courage My Love. He used to find any excuse he could to drop in on her, just to see her amidst the vintage lace wedding gowns, a drop-dead angel – and not this viral-sucking untouchable eating his insides out, lost to some soulless music she barely heard since the music was way beside the point and maybe that's why it bothered him so much.

He turns the radio up louder. That'll blow Quality Care's skirt sky-high. He bets the old lady's clutching the baby, nursery door locked tight as a clam, rolling her eyes back up into her head moaning, Animals. Lee'll go for that.

He goes to the top of the basement stairs.

Lee.

Unless what kills him the most is this: he doesn't even know what lap dancing is, being too embarrassed to ask.

Lee, he calls again.

Lee doesn't answer. He turns the volume back down.

Fuck *me*.

He scores a chunk of brie from Karla's fridge. He can hear it already: Baby, I'm just trying to establish boundaries. Or: Baby, I think you need more self-respect. Tomorrow there'll be a note on the kitchen counter:

> Curried Chicken Salad Sandwich
> Cappuccino Yogurt (lite)
> Apricot Square
> Blueberry Seltzer
> Help yourself!

He puts the cheese on one of Karla's blue plates, finds the Carr's Assorted Biscuits in the cupboard above the sink. The thick ones – they flake good as gold in the mouth – are gone.

Oinker, bleeding oinker.

He settles for the sweet Digestives.

Bunch of words lying in bundles.

The old lady's upstairs napping with the baby. Lee's still downstairs, dreaming of pussy.

On the radio, Robert Johnson, Blind Lemon Jefferson. Guys he loves. Bass lines thunk pretty yellow until he's yellow all the way down inside.

Anita. Pretty yellow hair. Nice little hands on his.

The back door sliding open wakes him.

He looks like me, Baby thinks. Or I could look like that. Nod hello to him on the street, or he'd put his warming beer on the table in front of him and clap: sure liked my last song.

When the intruder finally sees Baby – it takes a full thirty seconds for those glazed eyes to focus – he says, Shit.

Then, Gotta go.

An hour later, Baby remembers everything: the totally uncool Moxy Früvous T-shirt, the nerd-shoes scratchy and only half laced up. That look.

When the police ask, Can you make a positive I.D.? he denies it all.

Once upon a time in a happily-ever-after land of forever-my-children *amen*, he saves everybody.

Then he realizes (it takes a while but eventually he gets it): these people he's storying, they're laughing while he's standing bareass-naked knocking on their door.

He might be eating Poppy's Special – eggs lightly scrambled with some hot salsa, a little chorizo on the side. Feeling not too dirty and never really clean, feet walking toward where he's going to go and who he's going to be, at twenty-four a washed-out hard-driving man.

This song he hears like he's standing alone in the dark waiting for the spotlight to come on.

A door sliding open.

Classic Endo

One day in the swimming pool I spoke in tongues. The pink parts of my bathing suit began to glow: that's what the witnesses said. They also said my hair – which I've worn stylishly, brutally short for years – grew into long tresses like tentacles, but here the disputes begin. Some claimed my feet grew fins, amphibian green, flecked with gold. Others swore my arms and legs glistened silver like scales catching sunlight. Still others muttered about eyes like polished abalone, lips viridian O's of astonishment.

How it must have looked! They carried me out on a stretcher, but not before a lifeguard dragged my limp body to the edge of the shallow end, rolled me up out of the pool and tried to resuscitate me exactly, I suppose, as she had been taught in Bronze class. I opened my eyes, looked directly at her, and she blushed.

Thank you, I said, I must have dozed off.

In her nineteen-year-old's gaze, the cruellest presentiment: I was conscious but I couldn't move, I didn't want a fuss made, I was embarrassed – a newly middle-aged woman whose body had given out in the pool, knowing what old age would feel like.

Daddy used to say, Young lady – you're out of control, as if describing an irrefutable fact.

I was always his young lady.

One dark Sunday afternoon when I was five Daddy and I sat in the kitchen of our Moore Park house eating corn chowder, thick as mucus. I crumbled milk biscuits into it until it was thick as stew, and drank Orange Crush, my orange moustache annoying Daddy a little. He moved his unused butter knife half an inch to the right over the table, then back again. He cleared his throat. I continued to eat. The muscles in his jaw clenched. I put my spoon down.

Light bends when it passes through a medium, he said. This is calculable. Light passing through the eye creates sight. There is a code that will tell you everything. When you grow up.

My mother had died a year earlier, from diabetes. I remembered her only as a thing roundishly hard as the Royal Doulton figurine in the living room: her glazed eyes, my mother's broody trance.

Put out your big paw, Daddy said to me through an afternoon sky silky with snow at my mother's burial in the Necropolis, three rows away, he pointed out, from William Lyon Mackenzie's resting place. The other mourners – a progenitor or two, a colleague from the university, eyes flitting like birds behind thick glasses – had left. Holding my left hand in his, Daddy wiped melting flakes from my face. His hat furred white as he leaned toward me.

He said, We're in this together now.

In the spring, melting snow leaked through our house's broken Italian tile roof. At night my room brimmed with small swimming things while sly electrical storms gambolled on the lawn; the wainscotting inside the window rattled miserably through my sleep. Uncertainty festooned my waking hours: walking to the bus stop on my way to school each morning I thought buttresses on the nearby cathedral flew like rainbows; timbrels clanged in the sky.

Between lunchtime bites of toasted tomato sandwich (I was a girl with a stomach for a head), I'd repeat after Daddy: Light as the source of all colour, all colours travel at the same speed in a vacuum.

He'd pat my hand. He looked after me well.

On my way back to school only the grappling hooks of Daddy's pure science seized buildings as they threatened to lean, dissolve in something much like madness, like slicks leaking out.

Takes after her mother.

My aunt's voice thumped from the living room on one of her rare visits. I was thirteen, gobbling cupcakes in the pantry. I stopped chewing: what had she meant?

A sharp rap, probably Daddy's knuckles on the mahogany end table, made me gag on a lick of vanilla icing.

Evelyn, he said. I believe she knows better.

I did know. At Havergal College for Girls I performed admirably: by fifteen I could binge and purge with the best of them. Waiting for the five o'clock bus each day after school my high math scores blossomed on my lisping breath, constellations in the already dark winter sky. But I was coming to know something else, as well: not for me the usual achy doldrums of being fifteen with no place to go but home where I sputtered into clarity only under Daddy's gaze. In our house I shrank – from his hands on his hips, his stares; my growing body, hips loosening into adolescence. I was mute as my mother's figurine, boxed, in storage.

After school one cold day in January snow squeaked like Styrofoam beneath my boots. Behind me the tower and turret, the leaded-glass windows and grey winter ivy of Havergal College collapsed sullenly and sank into early night. A Land Rover carried off the last of my languishing classmates, waving weakly at me through fogged glass.

Cars hummed exhaust over icy Avenue Road, their interiors glowing faintly, and I imagined all the car radios in the world turned on and crackling, static flocking like crows above my head. If I listened carefully, turned a corner and my ears popped – if I listened sideways somehow – I would hear them, ghostly emissaries singing, tremulous at first then jangly: destiny, aliens, something out there.

Barring that, a somewhere else I could be.

I remember the summer I turned seventeen. The fast car I stepped into. I'd become a fast girl with good hands, the boy breathless next to me, mouth slightly agape, braces glinting in moonlight. I couldn't chart that, make velocity-time graphs of the million stars at night above the fields of uncut hay.

I'd sneak home after midnight through the neighbour's garden so Daddy wouldn't hear the car engine. Pat Jimmy, the neighbour's boxer who slept outside in summer.

She'll break your heart some day, the brittle aunt told Daddy years before.

By my thirty-ninth birthday – in the end it was the aunt who moved in to take care of him – I suppose it was true.

When Daddy died I joined the central YMCA and learned how to swim. Day after day I lay on my back in the beginners' lane and fluttered up and down. The skylights were what I imagined cancer cells would look like under Daddy's microscope, puffy marshmallows poised to yield their geometric niceties. I gave up swimming and joined the beginner fitness class instead.

Three days a week at noon I leave my St. Charles Street office to walk past the shimmer of Yonge Street clothing stores, jammed with what I gave up wearing years ago, having entered the twilit zone of an uncertain age: no hard abs here. Hence, once inside the coolly sequestered foyer of the YMCA, the following elegant formula: grey unitard, black oversized T-shirt. Join the procession up the stairs from the change room to music swirling like mist. Twitch to Madonna's latest immaculately happy beat, until the instructor puts on a low-impact tape. Merengue like crazy.

See the two new girls, blonde, athletic – next time they'll take their lithe spandex-clad bodies to the intermediate class for a real workout – giggle as the every-Tuesday man rolls his eyes, sticks his tongue out in concentration, spittle flossing the grey stubble on his chin.

Shudder into an unconvincing semblance of Latin excitement past the pillowy mother who – free for two hours, three times a week from the spongy machinations of her one-year-old twins – mutters, If I wanted to merengue I'd take the fucking dance class.

Stretch. Curse. What works, works.

Imagine a rose clenched dangerously between my teeth, my eyes like daggers, my heart a dark mystery.

My clients – architects for whom I'm a public relations consultant – approve of this building.

Like Philip, in black. We meet for lunch at the restaurant upstairs.

A polyphonic discourse between a socio-economic dialectic and an essential, infrangible otherness, he might say of this building, probing his Belgian endive drizzled with walnut dressing. He is famous for this, duelling to the death those other clients of mine more thoughtful of the structure's neo-classical humanist contextures, its schematic reification of the non-heroic modality. Each encomium pins the utterer to a rabidly guarded theoretical camp, like an insect specimen jabbed through the thorax to a dusty case in a museum few would willingly visit.

Here you are, Philip says when I join him. He's already ordered. I nod: here I am. There is no arguing with Philip.

Well, he says, before I've opened my menu. Kira almost had a breakdown when I told her Jon was mounting Graeme's next show. Silly bitch. What did she expect? He's not fucking *her* any more.

At a single table nearby sits a famous abortionist, taking time out from the firebombings. Other celebrities frequent the place, too, from the CBC national treasure to the elegantly appointed diplomat-turned-publisher to the only slightly tarnished civil-rights saint – usually on Mondays, the YMCA crowded with those desperate to expiate the sins of weekend excess.

The doctor seems ravenous, devouring his black bean soup and apricot-oatmeal muffin. He licks the crumbs from the side of his mouth and with his fingers grooms the table for extras.

I eye Philip's leftover terrine with raspberry coulis.

Ken and Tony split up again, he says. *And* I hear from reliable sources Marta'll get fired.

Philip veers across the table, chin grazing his former appetizer. His voice drops, thick brows lean. He carefully mouths each word. Like my father, Philip fears I might miss something.

You know. *The Holbein disaster.*

The coulis, I determine, is delicious.

And. Amy wants you to come for dinner next Saturday. We'll do Thai, all right? Found a fabulous new source for lemon grass.

The skin around my mouth, eyes, tightens. My hand drags across the table like a dead thing. With superhuman effort I successfully negotiate my fettucine, loading up on carbohydrates limpid in low-fat sauce.

Philip pushes back from the table, elbows cocked. About Amy, he says. His wrists bend unnaturally. The man is all angles, like his old apartment, ten years ago, on Shuter Street, a monochromatic enclosure of limited-edition chairs, a Philippe Starck table or two. The expert collection of toys in aid of the studied deviance on the futon, underneath the Mapplethorpe.

Lacking talent myself (a fact I admitted long ago with only a few tears shed), I make a point of bedding brilliance. Though it was easier then: risk was the rage, every sexual act a code of transgression, a deconstruction of the ganglia of desire.

I was young then.

Like Amy. Philip's – impossibly – young concubine. Her fasts, *detoxification rituals*. High priestess of high colonics, she'll probably live forever; Philip, too, having found the fountain of youth in an enema bag.

Don't people just fuck any more?

The waiter materializes with a flourish. The good doctor has vanished from the single table. Philip turns down the usual latte and orders another mineral water.

About Amy, he says again, and blinks at his paper-pale hands.

She's pregnant. Thought you should know.

From the restaurant I wander to the pool viewing area, three storeys above a bleary grotto of water.

Here I am. Below, the lifeguards change shifts. Across from me, the director of membership sales quietly eats her lunch. Light aches through glass to this lull in the ordinary day: a hole in solid unimpeachable space to fall into.

A miracle.

Which is what I need. To be not what I am: doomed – to a small waist and large hips, a short torso and a round belly that will never ripple with the obscene number of sit-ups I force it through daily (at home, in private).

No escape. Your body, yourself, every micro-DNA impulse (I'd make Daddy proud!) drives you to the gym, the fitness rooms; to the squash courts, couples locked in an algebra of mortal combat, the rubber ball angled just so under the harsh white glare; to the dance studio, the stretching rooms.

Chunky with muscle, mesomorphs eschew the Nautilus machines on the second floor for the free-weight room on the top floor: fetishists with leather weightbelts, gloves, purists pumping two-hundred-pound bars.

Ectomorphs – ropy sinew twisting with each step – ascend to the roof to lope around a track, giddy with height and fumes from the congested streets below.

Endomorphs (that's me) swim to support an irreparable deficit of muscle tone; exiled to the subterranean depths, they suffer the briefest flash of exposure (though a plain black Speedo offers excellent thigh-slimming coverage) to become mere flickers, shadow creatures garlanded by curlicues of cellulite like speleothems gone berserk.

Realize your potential. Be the best possible you.

Be who you are.

This cave has been here a long time, Daddy said. Long before you or me. And it'll be here long after your children and their children.

We were in Texas, touring a cave after a conference Daddy attended. I was eight, on summer vacation, squirmy with white runners and white socks, white heat, humidity.

I pondered his pronouncement as long as I thought necessary to appease him. I looked over at the other children on the tour, skipping about our guide; maybe their names, strange ones like Bubba and Cleta June, made them invulnerable to the heat.

This cave, the guide said, then paused and smiled, as if she had a secret – even at that age I found her annoying – this cave is ninety-five per cent active. It's growing all around us.

She pointed to a toad lodged in a crevice.

We think he's been here twenty years. Probably hopped in when this was the only entrance for the surveyors. He eats bugs that fall in through the opening.

The other children crowded toward the toad, infinitely more interesting than clammy rock, and knelt in dust beneath a jumble of stone hammered by light from an opening above.

He can't get out again, the guide said.

Daddy held my shoulders. We gazed at the ceiling, the walls where the guide shone her flashlight at fossils, clay banks, places turning black and greasy from people's touch. In the close air of the cave a clutter of elderly women, amateur speleologists from the Cleveland Second Mile Club, smelled of old lady sweat. Though they *did* know about caves, answering in unison when the guide said, What's the difference between a stalactite and a sta-lagmite? Showing off to each other, saying, Eileen, look at that, and Eileen saying, Oh, I've seen plenty of *that* before, up in Sweetwater. Flesh hung in strips along their swollen calves and ankles, crinkly, unsmooth as old wallpaper.

The other children crouched beneath the opening, light from above carving their faces. I turned to face Daddy.

Can I play with the toad? I said.

He shrugged his hands from the nape of my neck, as if I had failed him.

By the end of the tour I was tired and thirsty. In the souvenir shop half a mile above they sold grape Sno-cones and plastic paperweights you could shake to make snow fall on a Texas Ranger, in unabashed defiance of climatic laws. But returning to our starting point, the guide fussily assembled our group, pursing her lips until all stragglers arrived. A clammy breeze, Daddy's hot breath, rummaged my hair. Suddenly, darkness. A man's voice rose.

God creates mysteries. God creates order.

The ceiling smudged blue; a creeping rose latticed the bumpy walls. Listening to the recording, I rested against Daddy. He pushed his hip against me, put his arm across my chest, and pressed.

What I remember feeling next: Daddy and, despite him, something – myself – grown lopsided amidst a shakiness of breathing rock, spores of pinky light; a chatter of wind through limestone like the rustle of wings through an as yet undiscovered corridor.

Marvel, children of God, as you behold His house, the recorded voice serenely urged.

My head felt hot, then coolly hollow as blown glass, the sound of the voice slivering it until a shock of whispers seemed to shiver from my feet and rustle my skin.

Somewhere in there, the dark-cave heart of things, something I will always know: a father holds his hand out to his little girl and waits for her – a woman with a hole for a head.

Below me in the pool the swimmers looked hazy, indistinct beneath the membrane of water. Their small bodies looked like crazy fish pulling themselves up the length, along the veinous thread of black line on aqua tile. From above, everything seemed so slow: the lifeguards, legs floating over the arms of their high towers and every now and then a twitch of the foot, up and down, a briefly perceptible impatience punctuating the afternoon's *longueur* only to lapse again into nothing.

Nothing goes fast. Like waking slowly from a long dream. Like pulling yourself out of the pool, having swum a slow pumping mile: that heaviness in the legs, feeling your heart lurch like a bear greeting spring. So slow it hurts.

I always waited. Something rich, something strange.

Nothing happened.

Only this: my body – classic endo, irreducible though lovers and diets come and go – and the face I watch collapse with age, sucked inward, downward by this relentless science Daddy never mentioned: this catastrophe called gravity.

In the change room I stashed my DKNY dress in a locker. Removed my Bakelite bangles. Stripped to my lumpen mass. My afternoon calls could wait.

In the pool I licked the dusty insides of my goggles – unused a year in my tote – then pulled them on and tested the seal. One, up; two, down. Eventually, five and six. Finally, nine, where I touched the edge of the deep end and pushed off again, chest tightening like a drying plaster cast.

Heaving past the muscled legs of the lifeguard I conjured ten, the water's glazed surface hard as porcelain; summoning eleven, the heavy water held only an overtonal blast of bubbles trumpeting from my marbling lips – and this single viscous thought: *I'm going to drown.* Twelve, thirteen, unbearable fourteen. Being forty-two. Trapped in my ribs.

Then I felt light, unbelievably light, and fast. The water held me up; I could almost breathe it in.

Then the water closed over me. Dark.

Chain chain chain – I'm running in a circle, flapping my arms like an ungainly bird – *chain of fools.*

I work those glutes (fabulous glutes!), the Raylettes (so sweet! so beguiling!) teasing Ray: *Baby, shake that thing.*

Stretch it out, the instructor says later, during the mat work.

Grunting deliriously, chin yearning impossibly toward my left kneecap, I can't fully recall the time I fell asleep and dreamed strange dreams. When black wings – black as the black lines that tell you which lane you're sup- posed to swim in – pulled me up out of the pool, and I forgot my name and where I was. I woke laughing, drowning, my blood pumping chlorine. Angels, every- thing, last Thursday.

Reach up, the instructor says. Let yourself fall.

Maple Dawn

Need a tow? I'm drunk. I'm in my little boat. Whitefish is up, a dollar-eighty a pound. I let the nets stay down. Tomorrow I'll pull them in, or some other time though the year slides fast beneath canopies of foam and the sucking surge even in this place not ocean. Later this afternoon through my kitchen window Lake Ontario a wide field. Out the front door and across the road apples break in waves, ripple the ground. The sun something someone tossed away.

History is another thing: my father blind in the living room, in his one green chair. Anna; for years the old man sent for her. After, I'd take her back by the shed.

Late last fall the old bastard fell from the boat – out alone at night, no running lights, the radar turned off.

Never found him. Now only the green vireo calls at dusk. A false tanager. At times I'm too lost for words.

I've seen them with their sledgehammers and I don't give
a shit. They pound out the cotter-pin on a brass porthole,
slap a hundred-pound lift bag on it and shoot it up. Ellen
and Roy let them. They passed me yesterday at Main
Duck. Ellen got on the radio to say hi.

Need anything? I said. I've got twenty grand into that
old tug – I inherited good; why give it to the bank? –
though it's some investment, the way Ellen and Roy let
her slide.

No, she said. Just taking some divers out. Drop in
tonight. You and the Captain.

She laughed.

Well maybe yes and maybe no. Ellen calls me Leisure
Lance. She says, At your leisure, sir.

Later, rum like braids of rope dangling down my
throat, I saw the round white plates, cups. The ship's
bell, engraved: the *Manola*, really only a steel bow
section under tow to be welded to another steamer, the
Maple Dawn, that too finally busted up, in Georgian
Bay. Also a woman's mirror and comb. That's what I'd
have taken to save. Someone saw a pant leg inside a
rubber boot.

That one I don't believe.

Whatever else remains.

When Anna sings at the Regent I stay home. After the Christmas-tree fiasco when Vince shot up the goat he swore was sick unto death, tossing the carcass down to the ice, I said, Enough is enough. I'd got the Pathfinder stuck like a pig in the woods and Roy got the backhoe to tow me out; when we came into the kitchen there was Ellen and Anna looking. Anna said, Where's the fucking tree?

Anna called yesterday. She's got a show tomorrow night but won't be paid until next week.

Well?

Ellen called.

Reports. Sightings. They want to go out tonight to search but the wind's up six knots. Write this down, Lance, Ellen says. The co-ordinates.

The Captain strangulates my tongue.

I've got the relevant numbers, I say. I can't say no more.

Roy got her running early. I stayed home, thumbed *Playboy*, though this morning there is no delight. Sitting on the toilet I fumbled my zipper. All the things I can't find.

Ellen called at ten to say the GPS went down. Well? Well, she said. Just the old goat, bumping along the coast of Quinte near Waupoos.

Tonight when Anna comes from Cherry Valley for cash I'll say maybe yes and maybe no. Anna's a piss-tank so she'll startle, a way I like her to look.

To calm her I'll pass my hand over her brown hair,
push her down, *Down*, I'll say.

I want her to find what I'm looking for.

Testing, Testing

For a while – the time during which I thought surely I would die – I wanted to go back to the psychic. Better still, I wanted to call in the middle of the night and leave messages on her answering machine, messages designed to undermine at the very least her sanity. Somebody had to take the blame.

Can't you see?

And now. Now. What can I say.

I lived for a year in a house on Victor with five people, a Doberman, a German shepherd, a Netherlands dwarf rabbit (mine!) called Emily Dickinson, two peach-faced lovebirds, a kitten called Strobelight, and two hooded rats called Saddam and Saddam. I was living on amphetamines, it seemed. I sold, too. I sold some to my girlfriend once, who had recently moved out. The phone rang in the middle of the night. It was my girlfriend, saying she'd taken an overdose. Do I know you? I kept asking, until this guy who lived there – we called him the White Anglosaxophone, belittling his dream of becoming Ornette Coleman reincarnate – this guy gently took the receiver from my hand. He thought maybe it was an obscene phone call: in that house we seemed to get a lot – every third or fourth call almost.

What do you want? he wheedled into the phone. What is it you *really* want?

About the same time I lived on Victor I worked as a nighttime security guard at the Boulevard Club on Lakeshore Drive, with the Doberman. Most of the time I was jumpy. One morning two years earlier a guard was found face down in the swimming pool. Entering one locker room after another – men's, women's, juniors', those by the tennis courts and those by the pool – I'd loose the dog to sniff shower stalls, toilet cubicles, everything; everywhere, in fact, a dangerous offender might hide. I knew that dog would bite first, ask questions later.

The one area I liked to patrol was the curling rink. It was quiet there, cold. For this I kept the dog leashed, and carefully negotiated a strip of cedar decking from one end of the ice to the other.

And if I let the dog go?

I imagined the cuts in the ice from the dog's nails – the tracing lacy as the lines on a person's palm – radiating from a garbled centre where I'd whipped the beast to a frenzy with a tennis ball saying, Look, Daisy, Daisy want the ball?

The Boulevard Club: mine to protect, inviolate, pristine – never mind that every two hours or so I'd take the dog outside to shit in the flower beds. She had a bowel infection not even rice mixed with hamburger could cure.

Once on a moonless night when I'd been up two days straight, maybe more, my scalp tingly and tart with Black Beauties, I took the dog outside the club to do her business. As I waited for her to finish, I could dimly make out the marina sailboats rocking, the trees in the nearby park swaying. I could hear the occasional baying of what seemed to be every solitudinous beast of night, from the lost cygnet I saw jerking disconsolately into and out of the water to the stray Canada goose bruising the night sky over Lakeshore Drive. The lights of the city shone to the north, blurring with those from passing cars. Everything, in every place I looked, was speeding ahead, so fast I could barely catch the drift.

Then the wind lifted noise my way. It was coming from the fence between the park and the club parking lot. Moaning. Sex and love. Almost certainly, pain. As my eyes adjusted to the dark I saw a woman lean tight into a smaller woman. Then the wind changed direction. The dog was standing still, looking at me. We went back inside.

Once an hour I'd take the dog into the women's washroom near the main entrance and let her drink from a
toilet, counting fifteen laps before pulling her away. Any
more and she'd throw up. We'd wait a minute, then I'd
count another fifteen. That night in the washroom I
thought she wasn't bad-looking for a Doberman, a rare
blue instead of the usual black and tan or red though her
coat was coarse and oily to the touch, making her hard
to warm up to.

Coming back into the main foyer I could tell that
outside the wind was up again, wilding along the hallways and up the stairs. The tennis court workers, whose
shift ended as mine began, said it was the ghost of the
dead guard, and from the hue and cry some nights, a deft
Stockhausen caterwauling, I could almost believe it was
true though I tried not to give it much thought. If these
were messages from the dead I didn't want to know.

I tried to keep my mind on what I'd say in my nightly
report, though mostly I just wanted my shift to be over.
My ex used to meet me outside the club at six o'clock.
We'd sit in the car and drink coffee and watch the first
rowers of the morning eel across the greasy lake, then
we'd joyride the Gardiner past the Tip Top Tailors
building, heading east toward the Redpath Sugar stacks
along the waterfront. Sometimes we'd stop at Cherry
Beach and make out – two women in a place the police
would occasionally take a stray pro to bang for free. After
everything, home to Victor.

But now I had recognized my ex's car in the parking lot outside, had seen her bulk and heft lowering among the park trees. Every sliding moment, each flung thought, had ended, and as I picked up my clipboard from the desk at reception I felt crazy with knowing it: I'm coming out with my arms up, I confess to the crime, for god's sake don't shoot; and anything else that shook itself awake and came clear inside my head. I forgave her, I hated her, I wanted my girlfriend back.

Just as suddenly, all the craziness went out of me. Daisy lay at my feet, bleating mildly. She had to go out again.

I put the clipboard back and unlocked the front door. For a moment Daisy seemed happy, snout thrust joyously toward a tumble of stars and streetlights. For a moment, so did I.

The things I wished for back then! – that poor dog yelping in long white wheelies across the curling rink while the Boulevard Club ghost whooped it up and down the hallways like a wild cowboy, like a bad case of hiccups, like a cough that never goes away, recurring yeast infections and, finally, skin lesions, though I test negative, test negative, test negative.

The winter I lived on Victor I did whatever. I quit the security job. I quit adult-ed – again. I went out at night, sometimes alone, often not. During the day I walked the Doberman down Logan to Withrow Park.

My girlfriend was gone, gone. Once, somebody told me she got beat up at closing time outside The Rose on Parliament Street. Shortly afterward I thought I saw her on Yonge Street, and for that brief moment of mistaken identity I thought she looked all right. I wanted to call to her, but stopped myself in time: I knew the anger you could feel at being loved could far exceed the anger you might feel at being unloved.

So that was it: there was nothing else we could blame each other for.

My breath sent cartoon bubbles into the cold air. A woman with short hair passed me and crossed at the light. For the rest of the afternoon I drifted in and out of stores along rich Bloor, then doubled back, walking east through the cold eternal light. In the pink tea room on the Danforth the Oracle (Nancy) plumped and kneaded my hands in hers: I felt the need.

You are psychic in love, she said, tracing this line then that. Someone has betrayed you badly and this will never happen again. You will live to be seventy or ninety-five, depending on your diet.

Ninety-five, I thought. It would be like living forever.

You have great promise, she continued, scrutinizing each bump and whorl on my palm, though your talent is as yet undeveloped. You will achieve great renown.

I imagined jeroboams of champagne in a vast hall full of soft, mostly appreciative, laughter.

When, I said.

She told me I'd take many lovers in my lifetime and I confessed to engaging in the occasional sexual congress for the purpose of financial remuneration.

Hah! she said. *You see?* and her pug nose flattened considerably. She thrust out a slab of hand and pounded the eject button on the tape recorder. She hefted the cassette toward me through the roseate air. I passed her forty dollars, and got up to go.

She said, But only one will harm you.

I'd always thought of myself as a late bloomer, thought the best was yet to come, that I'd touched bottom and could only go up: any morsel my case worker might like to file, in addition to my high IQ scores and upgrading attempts, my new part-time job at mayoral incumbent Ruth Jacobi's headquarters: *onward with the campaign.* Flip the Rolodex. Answer the phones.

Promises, promises. Whatever became of them? All my life I was in such a hurry I never stuck around long enough to find out, and now the lost hosannahs of a lifetime drip tedium from a fluorescent sky.

At this point, what else can I say?

A long time ago, and a while after leaving Victor, I had a dream I was at the Super Save on Bloor. I was going on a trip, and I was stocking up on provisions. In one of the aisles I came across a storage locker in which she and I had placed our joint possessions – at least, the familiar objects from the time during which we lived our whole lives together. The idiot literalness of dreams! A pink plastic sailboat, the white plastic Swatch I bought her, never worn. Keys. The time I watched from the parking lot of the Boulevard Club as she pinned a girl to the park fence and all the sailboats stopped moving, and I thought only of a dog's ticky-toes in long white scribbles across a curling rink. Anything that promised to take me out of myself and give me something back in return, something better that could keep me going forever.

Then everything in the dream changed. I was standing on the sidewalk outside the Super Save, barefoot, rain soft as ion emissions (as illustrated in the physics textbook in the upgrading course I was taking), this funny rain leaking into my hair. As I stepped into the street a faint mewing, really just another of the feckless idioms of night, stopped me dead in my tracks.

Sometimes I think of that, and of how anything can in the end mean nothing, with not a thing in the world to bring us back, or even something to hold while we rock ourselves to sleep.

On my lunch breaks my glutinous tongue slowly muscles back a hot dog; my Obus Forme cushion takes my shape, and waits. Blue and white messages blare from the cinder-block walls. Ruth Jacobi Cares! For Changing Times! Until one day on the job, adrift on the sweltering calm of Prozac and cushioned by dozens of Post-It pads –

yellow, pink, lined and unlined and me opening and closing that desk drawer a million times a day – one day my test results will come in, negative, positive, negative, positive.

And what, all you beautiful promises, what could you say to that?

And love, what of love? – the human heart (mine!) ticking, ticking.

The dream about the Super Save ended like this: the cat purring softly in my arms, a bundle of pure joy, all I had left.

Lucky me, I remember thinking at the time. How could I be so lucky.

I take out a new Post-It pad, blue as sky, unlined. I write, Clinic re: test results – I write that one for me.

In this way I put my thoughts in order. I put my thoughts down.

The way I look at it that just about wraps it up. That just about says it all.

Except for this. I remember once I was driving down Pottery Road onto the Bayview Extension. Where was I going, middle of a moonless night? Moving, leaving that house on Victor, lighting out for parts unknown? All I know for sure is, there I was, the whole city glowing, spreading before me wild as thrush. I had this calico cat called Zebediah, with a crumpled ear from a bad case of

mites. She was perched on top of the bench seat, scared
shitless and holding on for dear life, right next to *my* ear.

That, that was something, I tell you.

And you, do you think I'm making this up?

Think. These are only the things you can imagine.